JESSICA WATKINS PRESENTS

YOU
Set
MY SOUL ON
Fire

NIQUE LUARKS

PROLOGUE
EVERYTHING WITH YOU IS SO COMPLICATED

Tone

"So, what does it say?" My moms, tried reading over my shoulder. "Let me see." She gave an impatient sigh.

My eyes skimmed quickly over the paper until they fell on what I was looking for.

Zero percent probability...

"He ain't mine." Relieved, I handed her the test results.

"Not that I'm surprised," she mumbled, sitting down at the table in front of me. "Now, you can work on fixing things with Erin." I watched her fold the paper in half and place it on the table.

I sighed, running my hand across the top of my head.

Yeah, about that...

"I know that look, Santonio." She raised an eyebrow, giving me a hard look. "Spit it out."

"I love E. I do. But shit wit' us is fucked up right now."

I shook my head. Erin was my baby, but we'd been through a whole lot of bullshit during the short course of our relationship. Shit just wasn't the same and she made sure to remind me of that every chance she got.

"So, you're giving up after you did all that moping around?" She smacked her lips. "Men are so stupid." She stood up she and walked toward the stove.

"Damn, why a nigga gotta be all that?"

"Because you are. You chased that woman and begged for a fair shot. And she gave you one even though she had reservations." She turned on one of the eyes on the stove. "Just so damn dumb," she mumbled, opening cabinets to look for seasoning then she slammed them back shut dramatically.

"What you mad at me for?" I pulled my ringing cell phone out of my pocket and pressed ignore.

"I'm not mad at you, Santonio. I'm *disappointed*. If you knew you didn't want to be with that girl, you should've left her the hell alone." She opened the refrigerator.

"I never said I didn't wanna be wit' Erin. I said shit wit' us is fucked up. She don't trust me no more." And she had every reason not to.

"And whose fault is that? Learn to keep your dick in your pants."

"Ma..." I frowned. I hated when she talked like that.

"Don't Ma me. I'm grown. I've been where Erin is at with your father." She shook her head. "It would be different if she could just erase your selfish ass from her life. But no, you went and got her pregnant. So now, she has to deal with you. I feel sorry for her. She deserves better than that."

"I got too much shit going on anyways, man." I stood up, adjusting my jeans.

"Mmm hum." She kept her back to me while she seasoned chicken in the sink.

"I'm 'bout to be out, though," I said, grabbing the paper and the envelope it had come in from the table. "You need anything?" I dug in my pocket.

"No. Just lock my door."

I pulled out a wad of cash, placed it on the table, and shook my head. "A'ight, lil lady, I'ma get wit' you later." I started out of the kitchen.

"Santonio, Erin isn't going to wait on you forever," she warned with her back still to me. "She's beautiful and smart. If you don't man up soon—when you finally do—it might be too late." Her shoulders dropped.

~

"He's not yours, so now what?" Erin rubbed her belly, tossing the paper onto her bed.

"Now, you ain't gotta worry about Amina."

She scoffed. "I've never worried about Amina." She looked up at me, and I licked my lips.

Damn.

Erin looked sexy as fuck. She was eight months pregnant and glowing. Her honey-blonde hair was longer and fuller, and her skin was radiant. Her tight sundress had her titties sitting up perfectly, torturing me. I wanted to lay her fine ass back and knock that pussy down *bad*, but she wasn't fuckin' with me like that.

I adjusted my dick in my pants as she stood up. "Either way, she's a non-factor." I watched her waddle over to her dresser. I smiled, shaking my head. Erin was having my baby. Damn.

"Whatever. I got tired of beating her soft ass anyway." She picked up an envelope and turned around.

I shook my head at the amount of times Erin had either whipped Amina's ass or was about to whip her ass. E was short, but she could pack a serious punch.

"Here." She handed me the envelope.

"What's this?" I took it from her and opened it.

"Pictures." She waddled back to her bed to sit down.

After taking the first picture out, a nigga's heart did a back flip. It was a photo of Erin wearing a pair of cut-up jeans. They were the only thing she had on. Her tatted arms were crossed over her breasts and she looked angelic. Her makeup was perfect, and I even took the time out to appreciate her pretty white toes. I stared at each picture, taking in all of her beauty.

Erin is having my baby.

My heart started beating fast.

"You like 'em?" she asked in an innocent tone of voice.

"Yeah, love." I smiled at her. "You look beautiful." I looked back down at the pictures. "When did you do this?"

"Like three weeks ago."

I nodded. "You should've told me. I would've come." The sudden feeling of guilt shifted my attitude. I should've been there.

"You were in Florida." She sighed, picking up her phone.

I nodded again. "I know Moms gon' love these."

"She already has hers," She stated matter-of-factly, tapping away on her iPhone.

"What?" I frowned.

"I took them to her at the beginning of this week." She kept her eyes on her phone.

"Why the fuck she get 'em before me?" I inched toward her bed.

"Because she did," her smart ass snapped, rolling her eyes.

"Man, Erin..." I let out a deep breath, remembering she'd been soft-hearted lately; crying over simple shit like running out of hot sauce even though she wasn't even supposed to have it.

"Santonio, I don't feel like arguing with you today." She waved me off, dismissing me.

"Who the fuck you talkin' to?" I was now standing over her, looking down on her pretty face.

"*You.*" She balled up her face. "Your mom has been here for me through most of my pregnancy. She was there when I took them."

I was gon' have to get with my OG. She hadn't told me shit about Erin taking maternity pictures.

"You don't call Moms for shit like this. You supposed to call me...*your man.* It was bad enough she knew before I did."

She frowned. "Here you go."

"Here I go my ass, nigga. You know keeping your pregnancy from me was fucked up."

Erin was six months and showing when I finally got the word she was pregnant. Imagine my surprise when I came across a picture she'd sent my moms.

"You can leave," she shot back.

Typical Erin... She'd rather run than talk. I was slowly getting tired of this shit.

"I didn't ask you to come here."

"Yeah, but I'm here." I glared at her.

"Why? Amina's baby isn't yours, but you still fucked her and more than once too. Since the baby's not yours, am I supposed to forget that part?" She mugged me.

"Man..." I rubbed my hand across the top of my head.

"Santonio..." She sighed, standing up. "Every conversation with you is an argument and I'm tired of arguing with you."

"Yeah, okay." I was over this corny shit with her. I loved the fuck out of Erin, but obviously, we needed some distance. I snatched my royal blue KC fitted off of her bed, placed it on my head, and made sure my keys were in my pocket.

"I'm out." I walked past her and out the bedroom door. "Call me if you need anything." I shook my head as she followed close behind me.

"I bet I won't call you for shit." We made it downstairs and she pushed me hard in my back. "I can't stand you!"

"Cool." Her little ass had some strength, but not enough to really move me. I ignored her aggressiveness and kept on to the front door.

"How many other women did you fuck that I didn't find out about? Huh?" Her voice had become soft, and I knew tears would soon follow.

Fuck.

Erin didn't cry. She was tough as shit and she refused to let anybody see her weak. It took a lot to pull her out of her element. I stopped in my tracks and faced her.

"Why are you doing all this?" I asked, truly confused. The test results from Amina's baby came back negative. I thought that shit would have her ecstatic. Instead, she was tripping, blowing my high.

"Because I wish I never met you." Her voice cracked and the water works started. "You don't know how hard this pregnancy has been on me. My best friend is dead!" she yelled in my face. "My man is a cheater and I'm pregnant!" Tears trickled down her cheeks. "And you think you coming in here saying a bitch you fucked with the *whole* time we were together baby ain't yours will make shit better?" She wiped her face.

I shook my head.

"You're so inconsiderate, Santonio."

"And you confused as fuck," I shot back. "One minute you saying we can work it out if the baby ain't mine and the next you trippin' the fuck out." I started for the door again. "Go take a fuckin' nap or something."

"Fuck you!" she screamed before I slammed the door shut behind me.

I fumbled with my keys until I found her house key, I locked the door and proceeded down the stairs and to my ride. Yeah, E and I needed some space. I had other shit that needed my focus, like this money. I had an empire to run and even though Erin was my queen, I needed a break from the melodramatics.

ERIN

After Santonio left, I rushed to the bathroom. I made it just in time before the Buffalo wings, and French fries I'd devoured earlier came spilling out of my mouth. Tears welled up in my eyes as I emptied out my stomach, making me regret letting him get me so worked up. Once I was finished, I washed my hands, brushed my teeth and exited the bathroom with a full-blown attitude. How dare he?

Waving the test results in my face did *not* erase the heartache I'd endured because of his constant deceit. I couldn't wait to call Sasha and Skyy to tell on him. Making my way through my home, I made sure all of the lights were cut off before I started climbing the marble stairs back up to my bedroom. The emptiness of my house made me emotional. I was expecting my first baby by the only man I'd ever love and I was all alone. I stopped at my daughter's nursery and cut the light on and glanced around.

Sanaa was coming *soon*, and I was terrified and unprepared. After, entering her room, I went to stand in front of the wide bay window. I ran my hands across the purple, glittery window sill and smiled.

Sanaa is coming.

My smile dropped quickly as I watched Tone's red Ashton Martin pull back into my wrap-around driveway. He climbed out the car and rushed up the walkway in a hurry. I stepped away from the window and made my exit, not bothering to cut the light off. My red-wine faux fur house slippers flopped against the floor as I made my way *back* downstairs. Once I hit the landing, I fixed my dress.

I opened the door and frowned. "Quit banging on my damn door."

"Man." He sighed, picking me up bridal style. Closing the door with his foot, he carried me towards my living room.

"Santonio…" I whined. "What are you doing?" I asked as we entered the room. Thanks to the lights from the front of my home cascading through the white, sheer curtains, he was able to find his way to the sectional.

He laid me down gently and started easing my dress up my thighs and over my ass.

"Santonio…"

"E, shut the fuck up," he said in a rough voice that cut through the darkness.

"*You* shut up!" I tried to move from underneath him, but he pinned me down.

"Why are you so difficult?" He planted a wet kiss on my neck that sent an instant chill through my chest. "Huh?" he asked, resting a pillow behind my head.

"'Cause, I hate you." I lied.

"What I tell you about that lying shit?" He rubbed the head of his dick up and down my pussy. I opened my legs wider to give him full access to my love. I felt him feeling me up, inch by inch, slowly as my juices slid down my ass crack. "Mmmm…" I moaned into his mouth.

"I love you, baby." He stroked me gently.

"Ooh, Tone…" Whimpering, I opened my legs wider, giving him the okay to go deeper.

"I want you and my daughter, Erin." His pace picked up.

I wrapped my arms around his neck. "Baby…"

"I wanna come home, E." He pushed my legs back, going harder.

"Ssshiit! Oh my God!" My eyes rolled to the back of my head.

"You love me?" His tone of voice changed. Santonio sounded desperate for my answer.

Of course, I loved him. Besides Sanaa, he was all I ever thought about. They were all I needed. No matter how much I couldn't stand him, I loved his ass a whole lot. My answer must not have come quick enough, because he pushed my legs back further, digging deeper.

"You love, Daddy?" he asked against my lips.

"Y-yesss," I surrendered, unashamed as my legs started shaking. "Baby..."

He pulled out tapping his heavy dick on my clit as I released a well needed nut on my brand new couch and all over his stomach. Before I could get done squirting, he was filling me back up.

"I'ma do better, baby," he promised.

Tears filled my eyes. I wanted to believe him, but I knew Tone so I knew better. He made promises he couldn't keep, and staying faithful to me was one of them.

He slowed down his pace, placing delicate kisses all over my face. "Stop crying." His voice went soft. "I know I fucked up," he confessed, rotating his hips as he slid in and out of me.

The urge to pee came again, and I braced myself for another orgasm.

"Aaargh!" My legs shook violently as he pulled out of me.

"You sexy as fuck." He watched me cum, stroking his manhood.

"Fuuuuck." I tried to control my body as he lifted me up gently and turned me around, positioning me on my hands and knees.

Plunging into my wetness, he grabbed a fist full of my hair and pulled my head back.

"Is this what you needed?" he asked in my ear before licking all over my neck.

"Yesss, baby. Yes!" I cried out. "I love you, Santonio."

"I know you do," he mumbled. "I love you too, baby."

"I'm cumming again, baby." I tried scooting away from the pounding he was putting on my kitty.

"Nah, bring that ass here." He brought me right back, and I started cumming.

"Wait!" I begged.

But he didn't. Instead, he fucked me harder...damn near senseless.

They say forgive and forget, right?

1

TWO AND A HALF YEARS LATER…

Why do you make it hard to love you?

Erin

With a basket of Sanaa and Toni's laundry in hand, I descended the staircase. My home was quiet, well, with the exception of Khalid and H.E.R's "This Way" playing softly from the stereo system in the living room. Sanaa and Toni were with their daddy, leaving me all alone for the weekend. I had no plans either. Maybe I could catch up on some reading, but other than that, I was going to use the alone time to recuperate from being a mommy all week.

Santonio usually only took Sanaa every weekend, so when he asked for Toni too I was shocked. She was only a few months and a damn spoiled brat. At first, I told him no, she couldn't go. It wasn't because I didn't believe Santonio couldn't handle her alone. It was because I knew by Saturday night he'd be dropping her off with his mama. Unlike Sanaa, Toni was a mama's girl.

I started the washer, swaying my head to the music.

I need to get out of this house.

But who would I go out with and where would we go? Ava was in New York, and Chance had her god babies for the weekend. My best friend, Sasha, and I hadn't been talking lately and Skyy moved down south last year. I shook my head, pouring detergent into the washer. I finally had a weekend to myself, but I wanted to call Santonio and pick up my ladybugs.

After loading the washer, I ended up in the kitchen making me a drink. Destiny Child's "If" was now playing, and I was just about to mix Coke with my Henny when my phone sounded off. I sat the bottle down and made my way over to the kitchen table and picked up my iPhone.

See...

Shaking my head, I answered with an attitude. I couldn't help it. The man's existence annoyed the fuck out of me.

"What, Santonio?"

"What you doin'?" Sadly, his rugged, raspy baritone still did something to me.

I rolled my eyes and headed back to the counter. "I'm chillin'. What's up? Where are my babies?"

"I just dropped 'em off with Ma Duke."

I smacked my lips. "Why? You just picked them up a couple of hours ago."

"I got some shit I gotta take care of, E. *Damn.*"

"Okay. So, what do you want?"

"I wanna take you out." He chuckled. "Since we both kid free and what not."

Really, Santonio?

Shaking my head, I put him on speaker, sat my phone down, and continued making my drink. "I don't wanna go out with you." I couldn't stand his ass, and he knew that. He was trying to be funny.

"Why not?"

"Why would I?" I'd made it perfectly clear I was done the last time we broke it off. I couldn't keep doing the back and forth with him. We weren't even together when I stupidly got pregnant with Toni.

"Man..." he drawled. "I'm sliding through anyways."

I shook my head before taking a long drink.

He continued. "You ain't doing shit else. Let me take you out to eat. You told Ma Duke you wanted to do that trap and paint shit. I made a reservation for just you and me."

Tone's mother felt deep down he and I were meant to be. Some shit about our stars not being aligned right now. She claimed she'd never seen her son so deeply in love. He could keep his "love" for all I cared because I hadn't gained anything from it but constant migraines. Things with Santonio and I were complicated...*too* complicated for us to have our happily ever after. I'd almost convinced her I was done with his cheating, some-timing ass, and then I went and I got pregnant again.

I reached for the bottle of Hennessy. "Don't waste your time driving all the way over here." I unscrewed the cap. "And you're not kid free."

Dumb ass...

"I am for the next four hours. So, get dressed," he insisted.

"No," I snapped in finality, filling up my glass. "Take one of your many bitches. You know I don't even fuck wit' you like that."

The line went silent. If I knew Santonio, he was trying to choose his next words wisely. But I also knew he had a smart-ass mouth. That's why I wasn't surprised when he mumbled, "I hope my daughters don't get your fucked up attitude, yo."

The nerve of this nigga... I only had a fucked up attitude because he brought it out of me. *He* had done this to us. *He* had taken me for granted. Yet, somehow, whenever he didn't get his way *I* was the one who was wrong.

Not feeding into his bullshit, I hung up in his face. I left my phone right on the counter, picked up my glass, and headed out back to sit on the patio. I was careful to leave the door cracked before I sat down and started I bobbing my head to the music. The high deck overlooked the backyard, and thanks to my brother, Eli, my lawn stayed neatly manicured. His landscaping company was booked for the year, but he was always had a worker come and upgrade something in my front and back yards.

A cool breeze swept over me, so I decided to light the fire pit. I sat my drink down and spun around to run in the house to change the music first. When I stepped inside, I thought I heard my front door close. Tilting my head, I frowned. Quickly going to the butcher's block near the sink, I snatched out the biggest knife. I made my way out the kitchen and headed down the hallway.

When I cut the corner to the hall leading to the front door, Santonio was coming down the hallway towards me. I stopped in my tracks and his 6'4" frame swaggered in my direction. You would think because he was a whole foot taller than me I'd be intimidated by him a little but *nope.*

"What you got a knife for?" He smiled. That damn dimple I loved so much appeared on his face and his pearly whites, two perfect rows of teeth, formed in a sexy smile. His tongue swiped across his juicy bottom lip when his hazel orbs washed over me.

"I have an intruder in my house." I eyed him as he turned his blue KC fitted hat backwards.

Pulling his beard in between his index and thumb, he widened his stance and crossed his free arm across his chest. "A'ight, killa." Santonio stared down at me. Our eyes got stuck on each other for a moment. When he smirked, I smacked my lips and broke my gaze.

"What are you doing here?" My eyes roamed his big arms. Just like ninety-nine percent of his body, they were covered in ink. The hand he was casually stroking his beard with had "Erin" tattooed on it in big, bold, red cursive letters. When I asked him why he'd gotten it, he told me to go listen to "Right Hand" by Drake. He said it was corny, but the first time he heard it he automatically thought about me.

"I told you to get dressed." He frowned.

I gave him the same look. "And I told you *no.*" I turned back around and began my journey to return to the back of my home.

Santonio sucked his teeth and followed me. "Why you gotta be so fuckin' difficult?"

"*I'm* the difficult one?" I shook my head. "Can you leave the way you came?"

"I ain't going nowhere. Ma Duke told me you been cooped up in the house."

We entered the kitchen and I went to put the knife back up before I actually used it. Spinning around, I crossed my arms and looked him over. He was dressed down in a white Saint Laurent tee, and denim jeans. The blue, black, and white 13's on his feet looked fresh out of the box as usual. And even though he was still standing in the doorway, I could smell his Tom Ford cologne.

"Tell Sadee to stop telling my business." I pushed off the counter. I loved Tone's mother like she was my own, but sometimes she pissed me off. I didn't want Santonio to know anything about my personal life. It was bad enough I had to share kids with him; I was stuck with Tone for life.

TONE

Biting down on my bottom lip, I followed Erin. Sanaa had been the one to spread her hips, but Toni had plumped that ass up. She was wearing a tight, yellow T-shirt dress with checkered sides and a pair of checkered Vans. Her dark, blonde hair was pulled up high into a loose ponytail. When I had first met Erin, I didn't believe it was all hers.

Both of her arms were covered in ink, and just recently, she'd finished the sleeve on her left leg. Her toasted almond complexion covered in ink looked soft and she smelled sweet. Once we stepped out onto the patio, I slapped her on the ass and she ignored me. Shaking her head, Erin switched to a seat.

I reached out and tugged gently on her ponytail, only for her to turn around and grill me. Even with the permanent mean mug on her face, she was beautiful. Her lips were full, pouty, and shiny. I knew all too well about the pain behind her dark brown eyes. They were hooded by thick eyelashes that probably weren't hers, but they gave her a sexy, sultry look. Her eyebrows were always in a perfect arch. I'd seen her take ten minutes to do just one before.

"Stop." She spun back around and took a seat. Picking up a glass, she sighed when I took a seat on the edge of the fire pit directly in front of her.

I turned my fitted cap forward. "You already dressed. Let's roll."

"I'm busy."

I shook my head. "Busy doing what?" Gripping the sides of her chair, I pulled her closer to me. When her legs were between mine, I gave her tatted thigh a firm squeeze.

Erin sipped from her glass, ignoring me. She had every right to be mad at a nigga, so her attitude didn't bother me. I had betrayed her trust more than once and shamefully, up until recently. I had been stuck in my own selfish ways for so long that I'd pushed my baby away. I wanted to show her something different this time. I needed my family.

She stared at me. "Santonio, can you go?" Erin smacked her lips. "You do this shit every other month."

"Man, I'm tryna make shit right."

She chuckled. "No." She took a sip of the dark liquor in her glass. "You want some pussy." In true Erin fashion, she called me out.

So what?

I hadn't had Erin's body underneath mine in almost three weeks. I'd been dipping in bitch's here and there, but none of them could do it like E. She was a freak to the core and didn't mind trying new shit. Erin took ass shots like a porn star, rode the dick like a skilled cowgirl, and sucked me off like her life depended on it. Gone off that Henny she could go all night.

"I wanna take you out on a date."

She rolled her eyes, unmoved. "Yeah, okay. And I told you I'm not going nowhere with you."

I nodded, reaching into my pocket for my ringing phone. "Yeah?" I put it on speaker and ran my hand up Erin's thigh. She popped me when I went under her dress.

"Hi this is Reginae. I talked to you earlier."

Erin frowned.

"Yeah, what's up, shorty?" I tugged at my beard.

"I didn't know if I had the right address," Reginae said sweetly. "I think I'm at the right place."

Erin pushed her chair back with an attitude.

"A'ight. Stay right there." I stood up and went back into the house.

Erin got up from her seat and followed me. "You are disrespectful as fuck!"

I shook my head, still heading for the front door. "Shut up."

"You shut up," she shot back.

We made it to the front door, and I pulled it open.

"Damn..." She didn't say it loud, but I heard it and I'm sure E did too. Her mouth dropped into an O, but she quickly fixed her face and cleared her throat. "Uh...I..." She fixed her hair. "My name is Reginae. You're Tone, right?" She smiled.

I nodded. "Yeah." Stepping to the side, I gave her a view of E. "This is my wife, Erin."

Reginae's grey eyes turned to slits. "Oh...it's nice to meet you, Erin." She adjusted the strap on the shoulder bag she was holding.

Erin smacked her lips. "Likewise." Crossing her arms, she stared at me. "Who is this and why is she at my front door?"

"This is Reginae..." I faced ole girl. "Right?"

She nodded.

"She's the one who does that trap and paint shit." I pulled at my beard and looked at Erin again. "Since you don't wanna get out, then we're staying in."

Erin stormed away.

I opened the door wider to give Reginae room to walk past me. I knew once Erin's mind had been made, there was no changing it, so I had already told Reginae what time to pull up. E and I weren't in an official relationship anymore, but she was my life and the mother of my kids. She was too dope and way to extroverted to be sitting in the house doing nothing all alone. It didn't take much to satisfy her.

Erin was interested in doing simple shit like walking in the park. She took joy in simply people watching at the beach, observing how they interacted with one another. One year for her birthday I bought her a Lambo. Ma Duke suggested I put a library in the house with all of her favorite authors' books. I had Ma Duke go through her Kindle and send a list of every author on her reading list. Erin was more excited about the library than she was the car.

The Lambo was currently sitting in her garage collecting dust. Her library had since grown. Little shit like that only increased my attraction to her. My baby had substance. She wasn't impressed by my dough or my status in the streets.

I shut the door and led Reginae towards the family room.

"This is a beautiful home."

"'Preciate it," I spoke over my shoulder. This wasn't *my* home. It belonged to Erin and our daughters. E made that perfectly clear every time we fucked and she threw me out before I could even put my shoes on.

Reginae's heels clicked loudly as she tried to keep up with my strides. "How long have you two been together?"

"A while."

"Are you happy?"

I stopped in my tracks. Quickly brushing my thumb across my bottom lip, I turned around. Reginae stared back at me with her eyes shimmering with lust. I chuckled, shaking my head. I had to give it to the bitch, she was *bold*. "Shorty, I'ma only say this shit once."

She took a step back.

"Don't disrespect my woman. You're here to do a job, so do it and keep the talking at a minimum. The only time I wanna hear you speak from this point forward is if Erin asks you a question." I glared down at her. "Understood?"

Her head bounced up and down quickly.

We entered the family room where Erin already had music playing. "Set up right there." I pointed to the wide-open space.

Reginae rushed to do what I told her and I went to look for E.

I ended up venturing back outside to the patio where Erin sat comfortably in her seat, drink in hand, staring at the flames flickering in the fire pit. Nearing her, I turned my hat backwards.

"Come on."

She sighed deeply. "Santonio, why are you bothering me?" Her eyes remained trained on the fire. "Don't you have something better to do?"

"I don't."

She looked up at me. "I'm sure you can find something." Her stare hardened.

I shook my head. "Man, you always fuckin' trippin'. A nigga tryna do something nice to show you I appreciate and love yo mean ass."

Erin chuckled before taking another drink of what I knew to be Hennessey.

"Bring yo ass in the house."

"Or what?"

"I'ma drag you in."

She reached forward to sit her glass down. "I wish the fuck you would."

I smiled inwardly. Erin had more heart than a lot of niggas I knew. I wouldn't really drag her, but I'd pick her stubborn ass up and carry her, and she knew that. I loved Erin way too much to ever harm her.

Inching closer, I hiked my jeans up a little and towered over her. "Can you come in the house *please*? I want us to finish this shit so I can take you out to eat."

"I'm not hungry."

This lil' nigga...

Stretching my arms out, I reached under her thighs and wrapped my right arm around her lower back. Picking her up, I carried her back into the house.

"Why do you feel like the world revolves around you?" Erin pouted.

"Nah, my world revolves around *you*."

I walked back to the family room with her in my arms without any further conversation.

2

WHAT ARE WE DOING?

ERIN

"So, you want me to leave?"

"Yep."

"But I—"

I raised my right hand to silence her. "Just pack up all this shit and go."

Santonio sighed. "You wildin'."

Ignoring him, I stared at Reginae. "Thank you for coming and I'm sorry you wasted your time, but you gotta go."

Nodding, she started cleaning up her mess. "I'll just leave my card."

"No need to do that."

"Oh..." She began putting her supplies in a black duffel bag. "Well, Tone has my number."

I chuckled and my eyes rolled over to Santonio. "I'm sure if he needs you, he'll reach out."

The room fell quiet as Santonio and I continued to watch Reginae pack up her belongings. I usually gave people three strikes before I flipped to bitch mode, but I'd given Reginae *four*. I gave her the first one when she cut her eyes at me after Tone said I was his woman. She got another one when they thought I was out of earshot and she asked him if he was "happy." The third one was when she took it upon herself to turn my Bluetooth speaker off. Her fourth and final strike came from the attitude radiating off her.

I could literally feel her negative energy. Maybe it was because I was a little tipsy, but this bitch was two seconds from getting cursed out. As soon as she was sure she had everything, Reginae faced us and rolled her eyes. Resisting the urge to embarrass her any further, I crossed my arms against my chest.

"I'm sorry if I offended you," she said dryly.

Waving her off, I snatched my jean jacket off the arm of the sectional. I slipped it on and faced Tone.

"I want Mongolian before they close." I led the way out of the room. "Let her out. I'm going to get my phone." I then took off in the opposite direction.

He's going to fuck her.

~

"WE SHOULD HIT up True's bar after this." Santonio said before taking a bite of his food.

I wiped my mouth down with a napkin. "For what?" I wasn't in the mood to hang with Tone and his rowdy-ass crew. It would be a whole lot different if Chance or Ava were coming.

"'Cause I want you to rock wit' me for a few more hours."

I picked my phone up. "It's going on ten. Don't you need to go pick up your kids?"

He chuckled. "They chillin' wit' Ma Duke for the night. I told her I had a hot date so she ain't expecting me until later on."

"This ain't a date."

"Yeah, it is."

"No, it ain't"

"Then what do you call it?"

I rolled my eyes. "Co-parenting..."

He laughed and the stupid butterflies in my abdomen went haywire. A smile tugged at the corners of my lips and I looked away.

Shaking his head, Santonio reached for his water. "Well, we gon' be co-parenting all night."

I frowned. "I highly doubt that."

"I don't."

Ignoring him, I pulled up the text conversation between me and my best friend, Sasha. We'd been friends since grade school, so she was more like a sister.

Me: Sash, come to True's bar with me

Santonio reached for his ringing phone, grinned at the screen, and answered.

"Hello?" The twinkle in his eyes let me know exactly who was on the other end.

He leaned back in his chair and shook his head, smile never wavering. "Sanaa, Daddy will be back. I promise."

I snickered, knowing she was probably rushing him back. Santonio sucked as a partner, but as a father, he was exactly what every little girl needed: a strong male role model that showed tough, unconditional love. Sanaa and Toni weren't just spoiled with material things. Santonio spent a lot of time with our girls, so they were spoiled with attention too.

Sanaa was a daddy's girl to the core. Three days out of the week, no matter what Santonio was doing, he took her on little outings. It was always just the two of them. They usually went out for lunch somewhere, to the mall, or ended up at an arcade. Without even realizing it, he was setting a standard for our daughter. He didn't even allow anybody to curse in front of her.

"Tell Granny to give you some."

I shook my head.

"Put her on the phone."

A text alert from Sasha came through.

Sash: Not in the mood. Eli done pissed me off.

I rolled my eyes. This was why I didn't want her messing with my brother. When they went behind my back and hooked up anyway, I was hurt for a little while. Sometimes, they put me in the middle of their bullshit, but recently I'd just turned a blind eye. Eli didn't have one faithful bone in his body. Sasha was baby mama number three, and the latest, but she probably wouldn't be the last.

Me: OK. If you change your mind just come through.

Sash: OK

Sitting my phone down on the table, I stared across the table at Tone. He was talking to Sadee now, telling her to let Sanaa have apple juice instead of water. She must've said something he didn't like because he grimaced hard. I laughed, knowing Sadee was checking his ass. She was soft-hearted, but she didn't take no shit.

"A'ight, Ma. *Damn.*" He turned his hat backwards. "Put Naa on the phone." He paused. "Please?"

I laughed harder before finishing off the rest of my Long Island iced tea.

"Naa..." He sighed. "Daddy will see you in a minute, a'ight?" He shook his head. "Drink water, Naa. Daddy will bring you juice when I pick you up."

"She don't need to be drinking nothing this late anyways," I finally spoke up.

Tone ignored me. "Okay, Naa. I love you." He chuckled. "I love Toni too."

He looked across the table at me. "You wanna talk to Mommy?"

I held my hand out and he placed his phone in my palm. I pressed it to my ear and pushed my food away from me. "Naa-Naa?"

"Hi, Mommy." Her squeaky voice warmed my heart.

"Why aren't you sleeping?"

"I want some juice, Mommy."

"And I said *no*!" Sadee yelled in the background.

"Sanaa, if Granny says drink water, then you have to drink water, okay?" I couldn't believe I was trying to compromise with a two-year-old. I looked across the table at Santonio. "Daddy said he'll bring some juice."

Tone chuckled.

Okay, so what? My kids were spoiled. I couldn't help it. They were living proof that unconditional love really existed. Even though Sanaa was a Daddy's girl, Mommy could do no wrong in her eyes.

"Okay," she pouted.

I pouted too, and Tone shook his head at me. "Bye, Naa-Naa. I love you."

"Bye, Mommy. I love you too."

I handed Santonio his phone back. "I'm tired. Can you drop me off?"

Digging into his pocket, he shook his head no. "We're 'bout to hit up True's spot. That nigga, Ro, said him and Ava getting out too."

"I thought she was in New York."

"She got back this morning. Rajon had a program or some shit like that at school today."

I nodded, silently thanking God. I hadn't known Ava that long, but she was cool. She was all about her money with an I-don't-give-a-fuck attitude. She gave Roman a run for his money, which was shocking because I'd seen firsthand how he tossed women around. However, what I liked *most* about Ava was that she loved Rajon like he was hers.

After placing a few bills on the table, Santonio stood up. "Let's go, love."

TONE

When I pulled into the parking lot at True's bar it was packed. You would've thought it was a club instead of a bar the way niggas and bitches were posted up. Erin unbuckled her seatbelt, and pulled the sun visor down. I turned my music all the way up and opened my door. Going into my middle console, I removed a pack of pre-rolled Backwoods.

Erin opened her door and hopped out. She shut the door and I watched closely as she made her way around the front of my whip and to me. I turned my body sideways in my seat, put my feet on the ground, and looked up at her. Erin stared back at me, chewing a piece of gum as I sparked the blunt. I pulled her closer by the bottom of her short-ass dress, stuck my hand underneath it, and ran my palm across her right cheek.

"Why you ain't got panties on?"

She smirked. "Didn't feel like putting on any."

I nodded, taking a pull from the blunt. After exhaling through my nostrils, I handed E the weed.

"Erin!"

We both looked to Ava who was making her way towards us. Erin hit the weed and waited on Ava to approach her. When she made it to us, Erin handed her the blunt.

"Bitch, you don't know how glad I am you're here." Ava laughed. "What's up, Tone?"

"Sup, Av?" I lit another blunt.

Erin chuckled. "I ain't even tryna be here for real."

After hitting the blunt, Ava handed Erin a fifth of D'usse. "Why not?"

"You know I don't like him like that," she said as if I wasn't sitting right in front of her.

Ava laughed. "I was wondering what was going on."

"'Cause you nosey." Roman came up behind Ava and she rolled her eyes.

My gaze landed back on Erin as she took a long drink from the bottle.

"You tryna get whooped in pool real quick?" Roman rubbed his hands together. The nigga was competitive as fuck. "I feel like taking yo money. That nigga, Sy, done already lost two grand."

Taking him up on his offer, I cut my car off. Erin took a step back and I got out. I shut the door and hovered above Erin's short frame. Her eyes were red, low, and glossy, which told me she didn't need nothing else to drink or smoke. She must've read my mind, because she passed the bottle back to Ava and shook her head no when Roman tried to hand her the spliff.

I quickly kissed her forehead and took her hand into mine and started for the entrance. I greeted a few people as we made our way inside. When I stepped in the building, FBG Duck's "Slide" was bumping loudly. Gripping E's hand tighter, I led the way through the crowd as they started spreading like the Red Sea so we could get through. I slapped fives with a few lil' niggas from around the way and stopped at the bar to get Erin a Long Island. I knew since she was already drunk she wouldn't drink the whole thing, but I still wanted her to have something to sip on while she chilled.

Once E had her drink, I placed my hand in the small of her back as she led the way to the pool table. Her brother, Eli, and his boy, Sy, were already standing at one of the table's smoking. True was frowning at something Nisha, his main bitch, was saying. Erin took off and went to her brother. I played the back as they exchanged greetings and then she made her way back to my side.

True must've said something fucked up to Nisha because she started spazzing.

"Why do you always answer whenever she calls?"

Erin's body tensed up, and I pulled her closer.

"Chill the fuck out." True shook his head.

"No, you need to tell Chance to find her own nigga to bother."

"What about Chance?" Ava came out of nowhere.

"*Man...*" Roman drawled. "Don't start that shit tonight."

Ava was a firecracker. Shorty was trained to go whenever. That's why I entrusted her with the business side of my empire. She was book smart, but she could also be straight savage. I was sure that's why my cousin fucked with her so tough.

"Girl, I'm not talking to you." Nisha scoffed.

"But she was talking to *you*." Erin sat her drink down on the table. *Ah shit...*

Nisha smacked her lips. "Erin, I don't have a problem with you." Her eyes then swept in my direction.

I'm sure she looked to me because she and every bitch in Kansas City knew I didn't do that mouthy shit when it came to Erin.

"But you got a problem with *Chance*," E snapped, flexing. "So, you got a problem with me." Erin didn't need my clout to make bitches respect her. I didn't know if it was the tattoos or the mean look she always wore, but they usually backed down. It could've been because being related to Eli had her banging bitches all the time when they were growing up. Whatever it was, it was clear that Nisha wanted no parts of it because she knocked True's drink out of his hand and stormed away.

"Dummy."

"What I say?" Roman looked down on Ava. "Do I need to take you back to the bathroom?"

Erin laughed when Ava looked away.

"Who tryna lose their money first?" True started setting the game up.

Eli reached for a pool stick. "What you got on it?"

"A rack a game."

"Aye, Eli." Silas tapped his arm. "Here comes baby mama."

"Fuck." He sat the pool stick down. "What you doing here, Sash?"

"I was invited." She stepped to Erin. "Hey, E."

"Hey." They shared a side hug. "Sash, this is Ava." Erin pointed to Roman's lady. "Ava, this is my best friend, Sasha."

Ava took a quick sip from her drink and nodded. "Nice to meet you."

Rage flashed in Sasha's eyes as she glared at Ava. Her gaze then landed on Eli. "This better not be the Ava you cheated on me with."

Erin looked on confused. She was probably the only one who didn't know what was going on. We all pretty much knew Ava had fucked around with Eli before she even met Roman. Not on no lovey-dovey type shit, though. Ava and Eli both said it only happened once, which was probably the only reason Roman hadn't smoked him.

Ava sighed.

"Chill out, man." Eli made his way over to Sasha.

She held her hand up and faced Ava. "Have you fucked Eli before?"

"Yep." Ava smirked, unbothered.

Roman yanked her by her arm and pulled her away.

Sasha faced Erin. "Where's the loyalty?"

Erin frowned. "What?"

"You heard me."

Eli ran his hands down his face in annoyance.

"You're way too friendly with a bitch who's fuckin' my man."

Erin stared at her. "I didn't know. And Eli and Ava aren't fuckin. You see she's with Ro."

"What the fuck does that mean?"

It means that nigga, Eli, ain't tryna meet his maker over some pussy.

My eyes landed on Eli. Sasha was cool people off the strength of

Erin, but I couldn't allow her to keep disrespecting. He caught the hint and gently pulled her arm.

"Sash, let me talk to you outside."

"You sho right, E." She shook her head in disappointment. Snatching her arm away from Eli, she stormed away.

Erin watched until she was out of sight and then took off towards the bar with an attitude.

3

YOU LEFT ME THIS SCAR ON MY HEART

ERIN

After knocking a few times, I stepped back and waited for Sasha to come to the door. I hadn't spoken to her since the other night when she called me *disloyal*. I was a lot of things like moody, goofy, annoying, and maybe even selfish sometimes, but *disloyal*? Nah, I wasn't accepting that.

I'd known Sasha almost my whole life. She knew things about me I would never tell anyone except Tone. We'd been through a lot together, including sleepovers and crying over boys to dealing with the death of Jeanette, one of our close friends. Sasha was my road dawg and had once been my confident.

Nowadays, things were different. We barely talked and whenever we did, our conversations didn't last long. It made me sad to think we were growing apart after all this time and after everything we'd been through. Our friendship was slowly dying, and the sadness I felt from that was unbearable.

The front door opened and Sasha stared back at me wearing an evil scowl on her face. Even though she was grilling me, my best friend was pretty. She was what most men called a red bone. Her hair stayed in its signature jet black, feathered bob. Her eyes were what usually grabbed people's attention first. They were a sexy shade of grey. Growing up, nobody used to believe they were hers. Sasha resembled that singer, Cassie, but Sash had body for days.

"What's up?" She opened the door wider.

"Can I come in?" I wanted to cuss her ass out for being petty, but one of us needed to be the mature one. I hadn't done anything wrong so I wasn't even about to trip with her.

After pulling the door all the way open, she gestured for me to come in.

"Where are the twins?" I asked, leading the way down the foyer.

"They're with your mom. I was in the kitchen cooking." She walked past me.

"I'ma stop over there later so I'll get to see them." I smiled, following her.

Once we entered the kitchen, Sasha trekked towards the stove and I took a seat at the island. No words were spoken as she maneuvered around the kitchen and I watched her. When I realized she wasn't going to say anything, I cleared my throat.

"I didn't know Ava had fucked Eli, Sash."

She scoffed. "Erin, do you really expect me to believe that?"

I frowned. "Why *wouldn't* you?"

She faced me. "Umm...let's see, you hang with the bitch and let's not forget you're pretty damn good at keeping secrets." She glared at me.

What?

"As long as *your* ass is covered, you don't give a fuck about no one else."

Wait...what?

Where the hell was this coming from?

"I'm sure when you found out, Eli told you not to tell me," she stated confidently.

I shook my head. "See, that's where you're *wrong*. I found out the other night." Of course, Eli was blood, but I would *never* do Sasha like that.

Sasha chuckled, facing the stove again. "You gon' sit here and lie to my face. Wow."

"So, now I'm a *liar*?"

"Yep," she chirped. "Just like you lie to yourself every day about what really happened to Jeanette."

Stunned by her words, I stared at the back of her head.

"You and I both know Tone had something to do with it. You just act clueless because you love his dog ass. Nette kept telling you not to fuck with him." She shook her head, stirring something in a pot. "Now, she's dead."

I sat still in total disbelief. Sasha was coming at me like I didn't love Jeanette too; like I'd felt no hurt over her passing. Hell, I was *still* hurting. We all were. She'd been dead for almost three years now, but not a day passed by that I didn't think about her.

When Jeanette died, she left behind her four-year-old son, Kory. For the first year and a half, I had him all the time. When Jeanette's mom decided to move to Minnesota, she took Kory with her. Now, I only saw my nephew on holidays and occasionally, through Face-Time. I missed Jeanette and I wanted justice for her, yet Sasha was discrediting my feelings.

"Santonio had nothing to do with Jeanette's death."

With her back still to me, she waved me off. "Girl, bye. You believe anything that nigga says."

I nodded. "Okay, so what's the real problem?" I'd given Sasha her three strikes. At this point, whatever direction this conversation was about to take would be all her doing. "'Cause you went from feeling salty because Eli can't keep his dick in pants to calling me a liar. Why are you really mad?"

She spun around, and I continued.

"You've known Eli the same amount of time you've known me. I used to tell you stories about my *whore* of a brother. Bitch, we used to fight because of *him*. Did you forget that?" I pushed my stool back. "Nobody told you to go behind my back and fuck my brother!" I wanted to leap across the counter and dog walk her miserable ass.

When I found out Sasha was pregnant by Eli, my heart broke into a million pieces. Eli was supposed to be off limits to Sasha, Skyy, and Jeanette. They knew Eli was a father figure to me. They knew he'd been the only constant male in my entire life. My little sister, Erica, and I had depended on Eli for everything when we were younger. Sasha knew that.

But *still* she smashed him. Sasha had damaged our friendship with that one, but I'd overlooked it and took that L all because our friendship was valuable to me. She lied to me and said she was pregnant by someone else until I had to pop up on her and Eli. Now, here she was calling me a disloyal liar. The fuckin' nerve of this bitch...

"As far as Santonio goes, you don't think I've had to battle with his name popping up in her investigation?" When Jeanette killed her abusive baby's father, that's when our lives started spiraling out of control. Tone got rid of the body and told me to never speak on it again and I didn't. However, Jeanette said she was being harassed by a detective.

"Jeanette was my friend *too*, Sash. I cry *too*. I'm mad *too*. I'm hurting *too*." Her throwing that shit in my face was low and uncalled for. Whether Sasha believed it or not, Nette's death had played a huge part in the strain on Tone's and my relationship. I was already pregnant and showing with Sanaa when Nette died.

Sasha faced the stove again. "So, knowing that she fucked Eli, are you going to still hang with her?"

I frowned." Ava's not worried about Eli, Sasha. She's with *Roman* now."

"And?" She cut the fire off and looked to me again. "She had sex with my man and now, the bitch got the balls to hang around him."

"Ava doesn't hang around Eli. She was there because she knew I would be there."

"Then why did you invite me?"

"Are you slow?" I wasn't trying to be disrespectful but Sasha was pissing me off. "I. Didn't. Know."

"*Slow?*" She chuckled sinisterly. "What's slow is you getting pregnant a second time by a nigga who don't really give a fuck about you."

Whoa!

I got down from the stool. Grabbing my purse up, I had to remind myself Sasha was like family. "You're the last person who should be speaking on *anybody's* relationship. You *know* Eli cheats. He's probably been out fuckin' off on you all day, and your stupid ass is in here cooking dinner for him. Catch this newsflash, bitch! Just because you think being an unofficial housewife will keep a nigga, it *won't*! You ain't learned that by now?"

Sasha's face dropped.

"The shit didn't work with Shawn and it damn sure ain't gon' work with Eli." Fuck Sasha and her feelings.

"What the fuck ya'll in here trippin' about?" Eli entered the kitchen, but I kept a heated glare on Sasha. She grilled me back, face contorted into the meanest look I'd ever seen from her.

"And for the record, at least I got my own." I pushed past Silas. "Bitch!"

TONE

I pulled up in front of Erin's mother's house and killed the ignition. I picked up my brush and stroked my waves a few times. I was supposed to have dropped Sanaa and Toni off two hours ago, but we fell asleep watching Shimmer and Shine after Naa made me repaint her toenails. It didn't matter that she'd just gone to get them done earlier this week with her mama. Sanaa wanted purple toenails, so Sanaa got purple toenails.

Turning sideways in my seat, I stared at my girls. They had the same toffee complexion as Erin. They'd gotten her pretty hair too. The only noticeable difference other than their ages was Sanaa had my piercing hazel eyes. Toni had ended up with the same soft brown ones as her mama.

"Naa, you gon' miss Daddy?" I'd see her in a couple days, but that seemed like a long time from now.

She nodded. "Toni too."

I smiled. Sanaa loved her little sister and was very protective of her.

"Toni-noni..."

Sanaa giggled at me.

"You gon' miss Daddy, baby?"

Toni stared at me and then looked out the window. I laughed, shaking my head. My poor baby was gon' have an attitude like her mama. I hopped out of my G-Wagon and opened Naa's door first, unbuckled her car seat, and helped her out. I took her tiny hand into mine and walked her to the sidewalk.

"Don't move, Naa-Naa." I looked down sternly at her and she nodded. I then opened Toni's door, unbuckled her car seat, and picked her up. I shut the door the same time Erin's little sister, Erica, came storming out of the house.

"I'm so tired of this shit! You didn't baby Erin or Eli like this!" she yelled, slamming the screen door.

I shook my head, taking Sanaa's hand again. "Yo, where's Erin?"

Erica rolled her eyes. "She ain't stopped by yet. You dropping your kids off too? This ain't a daycare."

I nodded, helping Sanaa up the stairs with Toni comfortable in my arms.

"Hi, Tee-Tee." Sanaa smiled up at Erica.

Erica sighed. "Hey, Naa-Naa. You have fun with your dad?" She asked and Sanaa let go of my hand and rushed to her.

"You see my feet?" She wiggled her tiny toes around in her jelly sandals.

The door swung open and Veronica, Erin's mother, stepped out onto the porch.

"Erin's not here and of course she's not answering when I call." She held her arms out for Toni.

After handing her over, I went in my back pocket for my phone. "When was the last time you talked to her?"

Veronica shrugged. "Earlier today."

Dialing Erin up, I put the phone to my ear and waited on her to answer.

"Hello?"

"Where you at?" I looked back and forth between Sanaa and Toni.

"Ain't that some shit?" Veronica shook her head and carried Toni into the house. "Tell Erin to come on so I can go. Eli done already picked up the twins. I'm trying to go to the boat."

"You heard ya moms?" I quickly surveyed the block. "She tryna ride out."

"And I'm not babysitting!" Erica yelled. "I might as well have my own damn kids!"

"*I wish the hell you would!*" Veronica yelled from inside.

"Awww..." Sanaa said, looking up at Erica.

"Yo, E, hold on." I tugged at my beard, trying to come up with the right thing to say without being disrespectful. "Erica, I get that you mad, shorty, but I'ma need for you to watch yo mouth around my daughters."

I was getting tired of reminding these forgetful muthafuckas. Erin and I didn't cuss in front of our daughters so I wasn't going to allow anybody else to.

"If y'all can't respect that, then I won't bring my babies back over here and you won't have to worry about this feeling like a daycare."

Erica looked down in her lap.

"Don't talk to my sister like that." Erin spoke. "And I'm right down the street."

"Where you been?"

"Home. Why?"

"Ya mom been calling you." Swooping Sanaa into my arms, I faced the street. "Where you been at?"

"I just told you," Erin shot back.

I hung up in her face and placed Sanaa on her feet. I then waited for Erin to pull up. My baby mama thought she was slick. I knew all about her little date she'd had with some cat named Marco. Chance had slipped up and told True. I hadn't killed Marco yet because I'd been busy. That's the only reason why the nigga wasn't dead. Homie was definitely living in his last days, though. Erin was too if she kept playing with me. I couldn't fathom another man touching her and definitely not fuckin' her. Erin was a sexual person, a straight freak, so I knew she wouldn't go long without sex.

When her black 2019 Chrysler 300 pulled into the driveway, I descended the steps. Sanaa was hot on my heels. Erin hopped out with a smile on her face, but a gloomy look in eyes.

"*Naa!*" She held her arms out and Sanaa jumped into them. "Hey, pretty girl." She kissed her cheeks repeatedly.

"Hi, Mommy!" Sanaa giggled, enjoying the affection from her mama.

"I missed you." Erin kissed her once more before putting her down. "Where's Toni?" She looked up at me.

I hit her with a reverse head nod. "In the crib." Pulling at my beard, I gave her the once over. "Where you been, Erin?"

Rolling her eyes, she took Sanaa's hand and started for the house. "You have fun with Daddy?" she asked, ignoring me.

Sanaa nodded. "Look at my toes, Mommy."

Erin stopped to check her out. "Those are you flyy, Sanaa," she said amusingly. "Daddy helped you?"

"Yep." Sanaa bounced up the steps and followed Erica into the house.

Erin chuckled and then let her eyes roll over to me. "Why are you looking at me like that?" She crossed her arms.

"How am I looking at you?" I widened my stance and continued tugging lightly at my beard.

She sighed. "I'm not in the mood for your bullshit, Santonio. Just say what the fuck is on your mind." Erin looked towards the porch to make sure the door was shut. "Everybody else has," she mumbled.

"Everybody like who?" I asked with a raised brow. If Erin was about to tell me she'd been with a nigga instead of here waiting on my daughters, I was gon' choke her.

"Why?"

My body moved before my brain registered what the fuck I was doing. I gripped Erin by the front of her Nike shirt and yanked her towards me roughly. "Who the fuck you talkin' to?" I mugged her. Erin was getting to fuckin' mouthy. I understood she was mad at me for the shit I'd put her through, but I was still that nigga. My baby had every right to be snappy with me, but my pride and ego wouldn't allow me to submit.

Tears pooled in her eyes as she tried to pull away from me. "I told you about grabbing on me!"

I let her go and ran my hands down my face. Aggravation washed over me. "Where you been?" I asked one more time.

Instead of replying, she stormed towards the house and I grabbed her forearm.

"Erin, man..." I drawled. This shit was becoming too much.

"Just because you have a guilty conscience doesn't mean you can come at me being extra and accusing me of shit that you're out here doing!" she yelled in my face.

I let her go. "I ain't out here doing shit. You the one going on dates."

She stared at me, unfazed, which let me know Chance hadn't lied.

"That nigga dead," I said and then swiped my tongue across my bottom lip. Nodding, I chuckled at what I was about to ask next. "You fuckin' that nigga?"

Erin smacked her lips. "No."

"He try?"

"Oh my God!" she shrieked. "No. We're just cool."

The fuck...

Wasn't shit cool about the love of my life kicking it with the next nigga.

"Yeah, a'ight..." I headed for my G-wagon before I did or said something I would regret.

I hopped in the whip and scrolled through my phone until I got to True's name.

Me: Bring me that

I looked back towards Veronica's house and watched as Erin took a seat on the steps. I started the car, put it in drive and pulled away from the curb with murder on my mind.

4

ALLEGIANCE

ERIN

I walked into True's bar and searched the building for Chance. I spotted her at the darts game, laughing with some dude. I was switching towards her when I felt someone grab my left arm. "Damn, baby. How you doin'?"

I frowned, snatching my arm away. "Don't touch me." I snapped my head in the direction of who I thought was a stranger. When my eyes landed on his, a small smile crept across my lips.

He chuckled, shaking his head at me. "Still meaner than the boogeyman, I see."

I laughed. "What are you doing here? I thought you stayed in Portland now."

He swiped his left hand across the top of his head, licking his lips as he gave me the once over. "I'm here visiting my family."

I nodded.

I hadn't seen Hakim since the summer after our high school graduation. He went off to college to play ball and we lost touch after he got drafted to the NBA. We were really close at one point; so close that I gave him my virginity. We'd never been in an official relationship, though. Hakim had been a for-real male best friend.

That's the only reason I trusted him enough for him to be my first.

I knew he wouldn't act funny afterwards or run his mouth about it. We were fifteen when it happened, but Hakim had handled it like a mature adult. It could've been because he'd been sexually active since he was thirteen. Whatever it was, I liked it and we continued having sex until I met my ex, TreVell.

"Look at you, man." He chuckled, eyeing me. "Lil' E ain't a baby no more."

I shrugged. "Haven't been for a while."

"I see." He licked his lips again. Hakim's dark eyes pierced through me. His brows were knitted together, but his gaze wasn't threatening. His pink lips sat plump in the middle of a freshly-lined goatee.

Letting my eyes roam his tall frame, I took note to the weight he'd gained. No longer was Hakim the lanky boy from gym class who forced me to be his friend. Hakim was a man now. He was all muscle now but wasn't overbearing. It was more like in a body-lifting kind of way. I could tell he worked out faithfully, though. The tattoos on his chocolate arms were new too.

Breaking our stare down, I looked towards Chance. "How long you here for?" My eyes swept back in his direction.

"Until Friday. I gotta get back to Portland because my son has a basketball game Monday. I want him to put some work in over the weekend."

I grinned. "Hakim, you got kids?" I shook my head in disbelief.

He chuckled. "Yeah, I have three actually; two boys and a girl."

"Wow."

Hakim has kids.

"You?" he asked and then looked around the bar.

I smiled. "Yeah, I have two girls."

Hakim smiled back. "That's wassup, Erin. Are your girls the reason why that ass is pokin' like that?"

I laughed. "I see you're still an asshole."

He raised his hands in a mock surrender. "I'm just saying. You weren't this thick when a nigga left." He licked his lips again. "I like it."

"I'm sure you do." I bit down on my bottom lip. Hakim had always been handsome, but it looked like life had been good to him. "I'm sorry about what happened."

He waved me off and looked around the bar again. "That's life."

"I know, but I know how much playing ball meant to you."

He shrugged and brushed his hand across his waves. "I ain't fucked up about it."

I nodded and glanced back over at Chance who was now sitting with Ava. They were both shamelessly eyeing us.

"You know them?" he asked, making me look back at him.

"Yeah."

Hakim nodded. "Well, I ain't tryna hold you up. I saw you when you first came in." He tapped on his phone screen. "Save your number so we can catch up. Maybe I can get you out to the coast for a few days." He handed me his phone.

I took it from him. "I don't know about all that."

He chuckled as I saved my number. "You crazy if you think I'm losing you again." He took his phone back and then slipped it into his back pocket. "Answer when I call, a'ight?"

I nodded as he walked around me and swaggered towards the bar. I watched Hakim make his exit and then made my way over to the booth Ava and Chance were sitting in. I sat my purse next to Ava and then slid in the seat next to Chance.

"Who was that?" Ava wasted no time. "Nigga was fine as fuck." She smirked.

Chance giggled. "He was."

I rolled my eyes. "That's the homie."

Ava smacked her lips. "Quit playin', yo. You better smash."

"Ava, really?" Chance shook her head. "Just because a man is handsome, it doesn't mean you have to have sex with him."

"Says who?" Ava frowned.

I chuckled. Before Roman, most people would've called Ava a hoe. She'd told us all kinds of stories about her wild-ass lifestyle. She was like one of the guys for real.

"That's not ladylike, Av. Thank God you met Roman. What if you would've caught something you can't get rid of?" Chance sat her phone down on the table.

"But I didn't."

Chance smacked her lips. "That's not the point."

"Because it ain't one."

"Ya'll..." I chuckled. Ava and Chance bickered like sisters. "Chill."

Ava rolled her eyes.

"Anyways..." I shook my head at them. "Thanks to Chance and her big mouth..."

Ava chuckled, and Chance sucked her teeth.

"Santonio showed the fuck out at my mama's house."

"When?"

"Sunday."

Chance reached for the drink menu. "I don't have a big mouth. True was by my phone when you texted me. He saw "Marco is cool so far" flash across my screen and started interrogating me."

I sighed.

"Then he took my phone and wouldn't give it back until I told him Marco was just a friend of yours."

I couldn't even be mad because Chance called me right after that and told me True knew I was out with Marco. This was my second time hearing how it went down, but I'm sure she wanted to clear the air just in case Ava felt like she couldn't be trusted. I knew I could trust Chance. It wasn't her fault True was crazy. Even when she'd cut him off, he still found a way to force himself into her life.

Ava laughed. "True is a bully."

"Tell me about it," she mumbled. Chance faced me. "So, what did he say?"

"Verbatim?" I sighed. "*That nigga dead*'."

Ava's violent ass thought that was hilarious.

Chance shook her head. "Didn't I tell you? I told you Tone would flip." She looked around. "Now, an innocent man is going to die," she whispered.

"He better run like Forrest Gump." Ava snickered.

Chance cut her eyes at her. "That's not funny, Av."

Ava held her stomach, still laughing. "Yes, it is."

I chuckled. It wasn't funny, but Ava's laughter became contagious.

Chance looked on in disbelief. "Something is seriously wrong with ya'll."

"What can I get you ladies to drink?" The waitress approached our booth. "Hey, Chance." She waved.

"Hey, Lola." Chance smiled. "I'll take a Patrón margarita."

Lola nodded and her eyes skipped to me. "What about you?" Her tone made me frown at her.

Strike one.

"A Long Island." My eyes rolled over to Ava who was giving Lola a hard glare. She must've sensed the hostility in her demeanor too.

"And for you?" Lola finally asked Ava way nicer than she'd asked me.

"First, you can fix your fuckin' attitude." Ava mugged her. Lola shifted her weight from her right foot to her left one. "Bring the bottle of 1800 and a few shot glasses," Ava said, dismissing Lola with a wave of her hand.

I smirked.

"Fuck is wrong wit' these rude-ass bitches nowadays, yo," Ava fussed loudly.

Chance shrugged. "I'm not sure what that was about, but I'll definitely be talking to True about it."

"Santonio is probably fuckin' her and feeding her empty promises," I spat angrily. I was getting tired of his disrespectful ass.

"Mmm..." Ava looked towards the bar. "What you wanna do?"

"Ava, come on. True don't need heat on him right now," Chance said sternly. "The police that aren't paid off try to find any reason to shut this building down." Chance picked up her phone. "I'll text him right now."

Ava rolled her eyes. "I swear you remind me of my sister, Blaze."

"Blaze?" Chance asked, still looking down at her phone.

"Yeah, she's from Kansas City too."

"Blaze Santiago?" Chance looked up from her phone.

Ava frowned. "Yeah. You know her?"

"I went to school with her best friend, Kenya." Chance cheesed. "I didn't really know them that well, but we shared Morgan as a mutual friend."

Ava smiled. "Damn, the world really is small."

"Way too small." I moved my phone out of the way so Lola could sit my drink down.

After placing everyone's drink on the table, Lola rolled her eyes and crossed her arms. "Ya'll need anything else?"

Strike two.

"Bitch, get away from this table." Ava dug in her purse. "I'ma end up tasing this hoe."

"Lola," Chance interfered. "You can go home. Can you stop by True's office before your shift tomorrow? He'll be waiting to talk to you," she informed her calmly.

Lola's faced dropped. "I—"

"Bye," I snapped, cutting her off before opening my straw.

Lola stormed off, mumbling under her breath.

"*Ugh...*" Ava said, pouring up three shots. "Bitches be weird and mad annoying."

"So, what happened the other night?" Chance asked, reaching for a shot.

Ava smacked her lips and Chance smiled.

"You know Sasha." I grabbed a shot as Ava poured up another one to replace the one Chance had taken.

"Yo..." She grilled me.

"You don't need to be drinking that much anyways." Chance tossed her shot back. "You have to drive."

I nodded before taking mine.

Ava rolled her eyes and then took two.

"So, Sasha came here trippin'?" Chance asked.

"Yep." I sipped from my straw. "I guess Ava fucked Eli at some point and she thought I knew."

Chance looked at Ava. "You never cease to amaze me."

"Good." Ava smirked.

"So, did you guys talk it out?" Chance asked before leaning forward to sip out of her straw.

I shook my head. "Nah. She didn't believe that I didn't know." Things with Sasha and I were changing. In the past, we would've handled each other way differently. Her audacity to throw Jeanette's death in my face was almost enough to make me cut her off for good.

Ava sucked her teeth as she poured up another shot. "If I would've known your best friend was Eli's baby mama, I would've told you I smashed him." She shrugged. "It wasn't even that big of a deal for me. It happened one time...*once*. Now that I think back on it, I didn't even want his ass at first. I was tryna fuck Silas, but he was all over my home girl, Ryan."

Chance's head popped up. "Sy? Your friend had sex with Silas? When?"

"Why? You smashing Silas?" Ava grinned. "True gon' kick your ass."

"Ewww. Hell no." Chance shook her head. "Morgan and Silas are together and they have been for a long time," she said sadly.

"Well, tell home girl her nigga is just that...a *nigga*."

I shook my head at Ava's messy ass.

"Now, as for that Sasha chick, I can see why she's feeling some type of way." Ava looked down at her phone. "But she ain't got shit to worry about. I don't want Eli's ass. I don't even like niggas wit' dreads." She started texting. "Tell her I was only looking to bust a quick nut, and that's exactly what it was."

"Ugh..." I frowned.

"What?" She looked up at me smiling. "He ain't my nigga, so it ain't my problem."

This bitch...

I shook my head again.

"Anyways..." Chance turned to me. "I'm sure Sasha ain't cool with you hanging with Ava."

"At all." I would pick Sash over Ava on any day, but the way she'd acted had me looking at her differently.

Ava rolled her eyes. "So, what? We ain't cool no more all because Eli cheated?" She scoffed. "Bitches are mad dumb, yo."

"We're cool, but I need to figure this shit out with Sasha first, a'ight?" I stared at her. The disappointment etched across Ava's face made me feel bad.

She nodded. "I can respect it."

Chance smacked her lips. "You should sit Ava and Sasha down together so they can clear the air. You're in the middle of something you had no control over." She sighed. "That's not fair."

Taking the shot Ava had handed to me, I gave her a small smile.

Life wasn't fair.

5

YOU TOLD ME YOU LOVED ME

TONE

"You wanna talk about it?"

I looked up from my plate to find Ma Duke leaning against the doorway.

"You're sitting here all alone, quiet, staring down at your food." She chuckled. "What's wrong? I made dinner just for you tonight."

Every now and then she would cook me and Roman's favorite foods and invite us over for dinner. We usually didn't all sit down together, but she always had a plate put up for when we dropped by. I'd let myself in an hour ago and warmed a plate, but I didn't have an appetite. I couldn't stop thinking about Erin. The thought that she wanted to date other people was really fuckin' wit' a nigga.

I'd handled that Marco situation only to find out she'd been at True's bar giving her number out. I was losing my grip on her. Erin was fed up. All my bullshit had finally caught up to me. Ma Duke wrapped her robe tighter and took a seat at the table. I didn't even wanna look at her.

"Santonio..." she said softly.

I pushed the plate away from me and leaned back in my chair. Erin had a nigga pouting on some soft cry-baby shit. When my eyes landed on Ma Duke, the amusement in her gaze made me shake my head.

"So, what did Erin do this time?"

"She been out thottin'."

Ma grimaced. "If I'm not mistaken, a *THOT* is a *hoe*?"

I nodded. "Yeah. My baby mama is a whore."

She shook her head. "Boy, watch your mouth."

I shrugged.

"I told you a long time ago Erin wasn't going to wait on you to get your shit together, didn't I?"

I tilted my head, uninterested in where this convo was going.

"You need to give her space to live her life. Just because she wants to go out on a few dates and enjoy a little male companionship, it doesn't make her a *whore*." She frowned. "She's only twenty-eight. She's spent most of her young years holding down men who stomped all over her.

"I ain't stomp on E. I upgraded her ungrateful ass." I got even madder.

Ma chuckled. "Is that what you think you did? Upgraded a woman who already had her own?" She laughed condescendingly. "Boy, are you dumb? I didn't drop you on your head so I don't know what's wrong with you." She shook her head. "Erin didn't need you then and she doesn't need you now."

I crossed my arms against my chest.

"That's your problem Santonio Keith Morris," she snapped. "You think you're God's gift to women, but you're *not*."

I tugged at my beard.

"You think just 'cause you got some money, and a dick—"

"Ma..." I drawled, cutting her off.

"Do you not realize it's more to loving a woman than just showering her with gifts and laying pipe?"

I chuckled, shaking my head at her.

"Laugh now, but cry later, son." She stared at me intensely. "It's Erin who's going to get the last laugh, though. Mark my words." She smirked.

~

later that night ...

I PULLED into Quik Trip's parking lot, parked next to a free pump, and cut the car off. After sitting with moms for another hour, I decided to jump into traffic. True wanted to hit the strip joint up, and even though it was a Wednesday, I was down. It wasn't like I had nobody at home waiting for me. My family lived in whole other house, almost forty minutes away from mine.

I hopped out the whip, checked the pump number, and made my way inside. When I got to the register, it was a shorty in front of me giving the cashier a hard time.

"I know its money on my damn card!"

I sighed, shaking my head.

"Ma'am, the card keeps getting declined. I don't know what else you want me to do," the chick behind the counter said with an attitude. "Do you have another one?"

"I don't need another one, because this one works just fine!" she snapped.

"Sir, I can help you over here." An Uncle Tom-looking-ass nigga waved me towards his register.

I stepped up and placed two twenties on the counter. "Let me get forty on three."

He nodded and I left out.

"Excuse me!" someone behind me yelled, but I kept walking.

"Sir!"

I didn't stop until I got to my Audi.

"I know you hear me calling you."

"Shorty, get the fuck away from my ride." I stared back at the chick I had just seen trippin' in the store. "I ain't got no spare change, so take yo beggin' ass on."

She smacked her lips and I started pumping my gas.

"Look, I know what this looks like, but it ain't that."

I smirked.

"I only need to get to my grandmother's house. She stays maybe three blocks away. If you could just spare—"

"Did you not just hear me? Take yo ass on, Felicia."

Her faced scrunched up in anger. "You got this nice-ass car and you can't help me?"

"I *can*, but I just don't want to."

She scoffed. "That is so fucked up."

"You better go stand at one of them exits off the highway."

"Screw you!" she screamed before storming away.

"Is that how you always treat people?"

I looked at the pump next to mine and my eyes landed on a chick standing next to a white Range. I wasn't usually into chicks with dreads, but shorty was dope. Her hourglass shape, sexy lips, and light brown eyes made her smashable. Her peanut butter complexion didn't seem flawed, but then again, she was wearing a bunch of makeup. She smiled and her teeth were straight, which was important for me whenever I was about to game a bitch down.

Tugging slightly at my beard, I approached her. "I'm actually a sweetheart."

She giggled. "Oh, is that right?"

I nodded. "That's what I hear."

She smiled. "I'm not sure I believe that."

"Tone..." I held my hand out and she placed her manicured one in mine.

"Brandi."

"It's nice to meet you, Ms. Brandi. What you doin' out this late, shorty?"

"Same thing you're doing." I let her hand go. "I'm getting gas."

I nodded. "Your man shouldn't have you out here pumping your gas at this time of night. Somebody might snatch yo pretty ass up." I licked my lips.

She blushed. "Actually, I'm single."

"Oh yeah? That's perfect 'cause I'm single too." I stared down at her. I wanted to fuck Brandi *tonight*. "You should lock my number in and hit me up when you're free."

She smiled again and reached in her back pocket. I ran down my number and once she had me saved, I gave her a quick wink and headed back to my driver's side. I hopped in, cranked the engine, and sped off. Once I got to the stop light, my phone pinged alerting me of a text.

8165541249: Don't be a stranger.

ERIN

"Mommy..." Sanaa sat at her little purple and silver vanity. Holding a glittery, purple brush in one hand, she stroked her American Girl doll's hair.

"Yes?" I reached down to pick up one of her Dr. Seuss books off the floor.

"Can I call my daddy?"

I sighed, taking a hair barrette from Toni before she put it in her mouth. "Naa, it's late." I said, looking at my Apple watch. It was going on one in the morning.

Sanaa and Toni should have been sleep a long time ago, but they'd taken a two-and-half-hour nap late in the evening and didn't wake up until almost ten.

"It's not late." She frowned.

I ignored her and continued cleaning her room.

"Mommy, it's not late," she whined.

I faced her. "Sanaa, Daddy is asleep. You can call him when he wakes up," I said sternly.

She stared back at me. Her bright eyes fluttered slowly as tears pooled in them. That bottom lip dropped, and she swallowed hard.

Sanaa was my sensitive child. It didn't take much to hurt her little feelings.

"Okay," my baby said softly, making me feel terrible.

Smacking my lips, I went over to her bed and picked my phone up. I took a seat and watched Toni try to stand up and then fall right back down. My eyes landed back on my phone and I went to my call log. I scrolled until I found Santonio's name and then looked at a pouting Sanaa. Exhaling deeply, I clicked on his name and put the phone to my ear.

It rang as I got up to take one of Sanaa's baby doll's shoes out of Toni's mouth.

"Why are you always tryna eat sh-stuff." I picked her up.

I already had OCD when it came to keeping a clean home, but Toni intensified my need to keep the floors spotless. She was moving around on her stomach now and somehow, she always found her way into shit.

"E..." Santonio answered, his deep chords sent that familiar chill through my body.

"Sanaa wants to talk to you." I looked at Sanaa who got down from her seat with a smile on her face.

"A'ight."

I handed the phone to Sanaa and sat Toni in the middle of Naa's queen-size canopy bed. I then made her a pillow fort just in case she rolled over.

"Hi, Daddy." I'm not sure what Tone said back, but Sanaa cheesed.

I continued cleaning her room as she talked to her dad. Sanaa's room was usually tidy, so all I had to do was pick up a few clothes and shoes. I figured they must've used Toni's room to play in because hers always had toys everywhere. I could already spot the difference in my little ladies. Sanaa was my girly girl and Toni was going to be my tomboy.

"Cleaning up..." She paused. "Mmm hum." She laughed. "You funny, Daddy."

I shook my head at her when she started twirling. Toni started whining so I picked her up. "What's wrong, Mama?" I pecked her lips. "You sleepy?"

"Okay." Sanaa twisted towards me. "Bye, Daddy. I love you." She handed me the phone. "My Daddy said get on the phone."

Rolling my eyes, I took my phone from her. "What?" I adjusted Toni in my arms.

"Why they ain't sleep?"

"They took a nap." I started out of Sanaa's room.

"Can I come spend the night?" It sounded like he was in a bathroom. "I ain't seen you since Sunday. You don't miss me?" he asked as I flipped the light switch on in my room.

"No. The only reason I called you was because Naa wanted to talk to you." I made my way to my bed, sat Toni down, and flopped down next to her. She crawled towards me drooling.

"Where's Toni?"

"She's right here, drooling everywhere." She looked up at me and reached for my phone. I unsnapped the flap to open her onesie to check her diaper. "You wanna talk to Daddy." I laughed when she tried to eat my phone. "She can hear you."

"Toni-noni."

Toni looked down at my phone.

"Wassup, Daddy's baby?"

She started babbling in baby gibberish.

"I love you too, Toni."

I smiled.

"Say Daddy." I suddenly heard someone knocking on the door from Santonio's side of the call. "I'm on the phone." His tone hardened.

The line went silent. I waited a few seconds and rolled my eyes, knowing he'd put us on mute. Sanaa skipped into my room holding the throw blanket from her bed. Once I helped her into the bed with me, she jumped over me and to lie next to Toni.

"You sleepy?" I asked when she yawned.

Sanaa shook her head no and hugged her cover. I ran my fingers through her curly, silky hair.

"Erin..."

"What?" I sighed.

"I'm on my way."

"We're about to go to sleep." Toni rested her head on my chest. "Stay laid up where you are."

"What the fu..." He stopped abruptly. "Take me off speaker."

I did just that and then I wrapped my arm around Toni. "Yeah?"

"What the fuck is that supposed to mean? I ain't wit' no bitch, man."

I smacked my lips. "I don't believe you."

"Why not?"

"Because you're a liar, Santonio."

"I ain't tryna drive all the way back home," he argued.

Rolling my eyes, I patted Toni gently on her back.

"I'm on my way, E."

I hung up on him and snuggled next to my babies.

When I felt my bed dip behind me, I sighed quietly. Santonio was so damn hard-headed. This was why when I was pregnant with Toni, I rented a loft downtown for three months. If Tone knew where I was, whether he had a key or not, he was letting himself in. He never respected my boundaries and I was getting tired of it.

He wrapped his arm around my waist and pulled me close. Toni, who was sleeping in front of me stirred a little and then faced Sanaa. Santonio trailed soft kisses up the side of my neck, and then nibbled on my earlobe. My heart started racing when he slipped his hand underneath my oversized T-shirt and he tried to spread my thighs apart.

"Stop." I inched away, but he pulled me back.

He kissed my neck again. "I missed you." Santonio's hand slid up my thigh, over my stomach, and right to my left boob. He played with the piercing and then traced my earlobe with his tongue.

"Mmm..." a soft moan escaped my lips. His dick pressed hard

against me making my pussy hot.

"Come take a shower with me."

I shook my head no. Santonio already smelled like soap, which meant he'd probably just left some bitch. I tried moving again, but he pulled me right back.

"Santonio, why are you here?"

He leaned forward and planted a wet kiss on my lips. "I missed you." He hugged me. "A nigga's been thinkin' about you all day."

"Right." I rolled my eyes.

"I love you." He sniffed my hair. "I know I don't say it enough and a nigga be wildin', but I love you, Erin. It's not your fault I'm a fuck up," he whispered in my ear.

I shivered.

"I'm set in my ways, but I know you ain't gon' wait on me forever." He gripped me tighter.

"Santonio, you've already shown me this ain't what you want. You don't want me or your family and you don't care that I'm hurting," I said calmly. Long gone were the days when he could get a tear out of me. He couldn't do it and nobody else could either.

"I *do* want you and my family and I *do* care that you hurting. I know I got a fucked up way of showing it but I care, E."

"You love me, but you don't wanna be with me. You wanna control me...you wanna control my life. You know deep down that I'm just too much for you. My expectations are just too high."

He sighed.

"We have daughters, Santonio. I don't want them to grow up thinking it's okay for men to dog them."

He let me go. "So, I'm dogging you?"

I ignored him. Everything I'd just said and that's all he heard. Typical Tone...

"I can't let you fuck wit' the other niggas, E." I felt him moving and knew he was turning on his back. That's the only way he could sleep, on his back with his arms crossed like he was still in prison.

"Whatever." I fixed the cover for Sanaa and Toni and closed my eyes.

6

YOU AND ME COULD MOVE A MOUNTAIN

ERIN

W hen I woke up, my bed was empty. I lay still for a moment and noticed the house was unusually quiet too. I stretched my body as a yawn escaped my lips and then rolled out of bed. Digging my toes into the carpet, I adjusted my tired eyes to the light. I trekked lazily towards the bathroom to go take care of my hygiene.

Thirty minutes later, I exited the bathroom with a thick Egyptian cotton towel wrapped around my body. I then stopped at my dresser to get panties and a bra. Afterwards, I made my way over to my vanity and took a seat. I let the towel fall. When I heard the pitter patter of little feet, I knew Sanaa was coming. Putting on my underwear, I waited for her.

"Mommy!" She rushed in smiling. Dressed in a distressed jeans, gold Giuseppe high tops, and a purple shirt with "Shimmer and Shine" on it, my baby looked cute. Her long hair was in at least eight ponytails with different colored hair balls to match her shirt.

"What did I say about running in the house, Naa?" I clasped my bra.

"Sorry," she apologized and skipped to me. "You like my hair?"

I smiled. "Yes, I love your hair."

She cheesed. "My granny did it."

I nodded knowingly. Sadee was the only person I trusted to touch my babies' hair.

"Sanaa!" Tone yelled before I could see him.

"In here, Daddy!" she yelled back, trying to get on the seat with me. I helped her and she spun around to face the mirror.

"Go do what I asked you to." He entered holding Toni.

Her white onesie was tucked into similar jeans as Sanaa's, and on her tiny feet were Gucci sneakers. Her curly hair was pulled up into two puffballs and her Gucci headband matched her shoes.

Sanaa rushed past Santonio and out of my room.

"Sanaa Kelis, stop running!" I yelled after her.

"*Okay!*" Her squeaky voice made me chuckle.

Tone sauntered all the way in and took a seat on my bed. "How long you been up?" he asked, sitting Toni down.

I stood up and adjusted my panties. "Not that long." I snatched my phone up and made my way to my closet. "Where ya'll been?"

"Out. I got 'em dressed and took 'em by Ma Duke so she could do their hair and then we went out to breakfast."

I shuffled through my clothes. "Hey, Siri..." I waited for her to respond. "What's the weather like?"

"Here, Daddy!" Sanaa came back. "I couldn't find the powder."

Deciding on black spandex shorts and a cut-off sweatshirt, I exited my closet.

"After you get dressed, I'ma drop them off and take you to get something to eat." Tone leaned over Toni and started changing her diaper.

I took a seat on the bed and slipped my clothes on. "I was actually going to get my hair touched up." I checked the time on my phone.

11:06am

"Cool. I'll just drop you off and when I pick you up, you can just ride out wit' me for the day."

I turned sideways to look at him. It was funny how he'd gone all out his way to dress Sanaa and Toni up when he was only wearing a black T-shirt, jeans, and a pair of Jordan's. He smelled like Heaven...like Clive Christian, my favorite cologne on him. His waves were bussin' as usual. The only jewelry he had on was an iced-out Jesus piece around his tatted neck, the platinum bottom grill in his mouth, and the Rolex on his wrist. That's when I noticed the gold necklace around Toni's neck.

I reached over and gently pulled it out of her shirt and read the gold cursive letters attached to the necklace.

Toni

"You like mine too, Mommy?" Sanaa asked, making me look over at her. She held her wrist up, showing off a gold tennis bracelet.

I smiled. "I see you, Naa. That's real flyy."

She beamed.

"Throw on some shoes so we can head out." He picked up Toni and her diaper and started out of the room. Sanaa ran after him, and just when I was about to call out to her, my phone rang. Hakim's number flashed across the screen and I looked to the door before answering.

"Hello?"

"Wassup wit'chu?"

I smiled. "I'm getting ready to go get my hair done."

"What you doin' after that?" he asked as I stood up to put some shoes on.

"I'm not sure yet."

"You should let me take you to lunch. I'm going back to Portland tonight and I wanna see you before I leave."

Sliding my feet into my white and black Balenciaga's, I contemplated on taking Hakim up on his offer. Once I got in Tone's car that was like signing my freedom away for the day.

"Maybe next time." I sighed.

Hakim smacked his lips. "A'ight. If you change your mind, I'm not leaving until eight."

"Okay. Talk to you later, Hakim."

"Stay up, E."

I hung up the phone, went to my vanity, and picked a pair of shades. Siri said it was only seventy-two degrees, but the sun was out.

The fall weather in Kansas City was usually a hit or mess. Some days, it felt like my favorite season and some days it didn't. I headed out of my room and went to pack Toni a diaper bag and Sanaa an overnight bag just in case Sadee wanted to keep them.

Fifteen minutes later, I followed the sound of Tone's voice to the kitchen. When I entered, he stood by the trash can peeling an orange.

"Nah, I'm 'bout to head over to Mom's now." He watched me and swiped his tongue across his bottom lip. "Yeah, just hit Ro up and let him handle it." He balanced the phone between his shoulder and ear.

I picked Toni up out of her swing.

"A'ight, I'ma get wit' you later." Tone paused to hand Sanaa half of the orange he'd peeled. "You ready?" he asked, slipping his phone into his back pocket. He approached me tearing a piece off the orange.

I nodded. "Yeah, I should be able to get in and out. Morgan keeps her chair free for me between twelve and three."

Toni snatched the orange out of his hand and he shook his head. "Meany."

I handed Toni over to him and headed out of the kitchen with Sanaa walking next to me rambling on about how she needed her nails done.

TONE

After we dropped the girls off with Ma Duke, we headed for the city. I convinced Erin to go to *Eggtc* so we could get her something to eat. Since the joint closed at 2:30pm, we didn't have long, but I wanted her to put something on her stomach since I knew the birds at Morgan's shop liked to make drinks and shit. While she was getting her hair done, I was going to meet up with Ro so we could discuss business. His little niggas on the eastside had gotten into a dispute with some niggas down north and I didn't need that petty shit fuckin' up my bread.

"What you gettin'?" I asked Erin once we were seated.

She looked down at her phone. "I don't know. I'm not really hungry," she mumbled.

"Yo, you being rude as fuck right now." I stared at her.

Erin rolled her eyes, still texting on her phone. "I said what I had to say last night."

"And I did too."

The waitress came, took our order, and then switched away.

"So, what you wanna do when you finished getting your hair done?"

She looked up from her phone. "I don't know. Pick up my ladybugs and go home. I have a few new reads on my Kindle." She shrugged.

I chuckled. "You read that shit so much, you might as well write one."

Erin frowned. "Write what?"

"You should write one of them ghetto-ass urban fiction books." He laughed. "You live the perfect life for the shit."

She chuckled.

"Baby daddy at the head of a crime family, hating-ass bitches wanna be you, and you ain't gotta do shit all day but be a mother to your daughters."

Erin smacked her lips with a smile on her pretty face.

"You living the hood-rat dream."

She laughed.

"Write about the shit."

She shook her head. "Okay, for one, it's more than just a *hood-rat* dream. Most of those books have life lessons hidden in the pages. Majority of those authors might seem like they're telling the same story, but everybody's ending ain't the same."

"Seem like the same shit to me."

"All rappers rap about the same thing. It's just a different MC."

I shrugged.

"No pen is the same. No talent is the same. No life experience is the same." She shrugged. "But we as people are all technically *the same*."

I eyed her.

"Most men cheat. Most women want love. Everybody chases a dream. Side bitches don't know their place and broke bitches hate."

I laughed. "The fuck? You a rapper now?"

She snickered. "I'm just saying. No book is the same unless the author flat out plagiarized somebody else's shit."

I nodded. "So, why they always gotta have some hood-ass nigga as the main character?"

"Simple." She shrugged. "Tough love is the best love. I know a lot of broken women. And most broken ones don't have a father. Some don't have mamas either. The kind of love most women get from a nigga like you is unconditional."

I licked my lips.

"Y'all fuck up a lot, but y'all hurting too. *But* unlike y'all, instead of destroying you any further, we wanna uplift you."

"I read in a book one time that broken people love the deepest." I couldn't remember the name of the book, but that shit stayed with me.

Erin's eyes danced around me. "Imagine the man you could be if you truly put our love on a pedestal."

I leaned back in my chair, crossed my left arm against my chest, and stroked my beard with my right.

"Not to mention a hood nigga, with some fire dick and a phat-ass bankroll is sexy as fuck." She shrugged, laughing as the waitress sat our food down in front of us.

I shook my head at her. "Y'all women are a trip."

Erin unwrapped her silverware. "No, but for real, I think if I ever wrote a book, it would be about self-help."

I watched her eat, still stroking my beard. "Oh, yeah? So, what would you write about?"

She stuffed her mouth with piece of pancake and shrugged. She chewed with her napkin covering her mouth, and then she reached for her water and took a sip. "I want women to know that it's okay to be vulnerable. It's okay to feel like all odds are stacked against you. Don't live in regret because mistakes are irreversible. Usually, we make horrible decisions based on our emotions."

Erin forked her cheesy eggs.

"But you said it's okay to be vulnerable."

"I didn't contradict myself. People hear what they want." She took a bite of her food.

"So, you feel like you've made mistakes?"

She frowned, wiping her mouth down with a new napkin. "Of course, I have. I'm not perfect. If you can name one perfect person, I'll take you back right now." She eyed me.

"So, if you know people ain't perfect, why you be ridin' a nigga so hard?"

Erin chuckled before taking a sip of her Mimosa. "You funny."

That's where Sanaa got that saying from.

I smiled.

"You're the man out there on the field, but what about *home* with the people who're supposed to really matter to you? Them bitches will never love you like I do." She started on her hash browns.

"I know." I stared at my baby. "I want my family, E."

She rolled her eyes. "Here you go with this shit. Santonio, how many chances have I given you? How many times have you disappointed me?"

"Too many to count." I ran my hand across the top of my head.

She nodded. "You still won't even be honest with me about what really happened to Jeanette." Erin looked at me sadly. "If you wanna fix this, then start with that."

Erin wanted the truth about some shit she couldn't handle. I was protecting her. I'd always protected her and now, I was getting the backlash.

"When you can be one hundred-percent honest with *yourself*, then we can work on regaining my trust." Her shoulders dropped. "Until then, just focus on being the best daddy ever."

My phone started ringing, but I kept my gaze on Erin. Regardless of what E thought, I wanted her and I wanted my family. Yeah, mistakes were irreversible, but the love I had for her wasn't.

7

WHAT ARE WE DOING?

ERIN

8:31pm the next day...

"I'LL CATCH you next time you're in town." I shook my head at how dramatic Hakim was acting. He had gone all those years without talking to me, so he'd be okay.

"You must have a dude." He chuckled. "He's a lucky nigga."

I rolled my eyes. "Why I gotta have a man? Because I didn't drop everything I was doing to have lunch with you?" I stared at him. "Or is it because I didn't jump when you mentioned you flying me to Portland?"

Hakim laughed. "Why are you so mean, E?"

I shrugged. I didn't think I'd said anything mean. I was simply speaking my mind. I watched Toni scoot on her stomach. "Hey, you." I playfully tossed a teddy bear at her. She kept on moving.

"I still can't believe you got kids, man."

"Yeah, me either." My other line clicked. "Hold on, Hakim." When I saw it was my mama, I let out a deep sigh and answered. "What's up?" I got up to go after Toni.

"Erin, come get your sister. Her ass has gotta go right now!" she yelled. I could hear Erica in the background talking loud, but I wasn't able to make out what she was saying.

"What happened?"

"Her mouth! That's what happened. I'm tired of the disrespect," she fussed. "Her ass is fuckin' and she's feeling herself."

I shook my head as I picked Toni up. "Ma, put Erica on the phone." I dimmed the light in Toni's room and headed down the hallway. I wasn't in the mood to deal with their bullshit.

"Here, take this damn phone."

"Who is it?" Erica said with an attitude. "I don't feel like talking on the phone."

"Girl, if you don't take this damn phone." My mama spazzed. "I'm the parent, not you!"

I waited patiently for Erica to get on the phone while I made my way through my home.

"What?" Erica asked right before I heard a door slam on her end. "Why did she call you?"

"I don't know. What's going on?" Toni tried to wiggle out of my grasp, making me chuckle. My child hated being held.

"Mama found a condom in my room."

I frowned, shaking my head.

"E, I'm eighteen. If I wanna have sex, that's my prerogative. You started when you were like eleven and Eli when he was eight," she stated as a matter of fact.

I laughed. "Heffa, no you didn't." Erica knew how old I was when I lost my virginity. She was just trying to be funny.

She giggled. "I'm serious, E. I'm old enough to make my own decisions."

"But you're living under *Mama's* roof. You can't be talking back and popping off just 'cause you getting dicked down and you feeling some type of way," I informed her grown ass.

Erica had it way easier than Eli and I did when we were her age. She got to stay out late, spend the night with boys, and even had her own car. When I was eighteen, I was working at two different

McDonald's, paying rent in my first apartment, and saving for a car. Erica was a spoiled brat and I blamed it on Eli. He was the man now and he didn't mind blowing money on Erica. Hell, he was still sneaking money into my purse when I wasn't looking.

"I'm thinking about getting my own spot. I can't take her nagging me, E," she pouted. "I need freedom to discover who I am."

I burst into a fit of laughter and held on tight to Toni as I doubled over. Erica had some nerve.

"Erin, I'm serious," she pressed.

I laughed harder. Real life tears burned in my eyes as I put Toni in her swing and took a seat at one of the tables in my library.

Erica smacked her lips. "You and Eli are so annoying, bro."

Wiping my face, I blew out a deep breath and shook my head, truly entertained. I'm sure if she had this same conversation with Eli, he and I were going to have a good laugh when he came by tomorrow.

"What's so funny?"

I cleared my throat. "For one, *Erica*, you don't have a job."

"So?"

I looked down at my phone even though I couldn't see her. She couldn't be for real. Erica was at the top of her graduating class, so I was sure she was just speaking out of anger. She was too smart for half of the dumb shit that came out of her mouth sometimes. After putting her on speaker, I sat the phone down and crossed my legs in the chair.

"How are you going to pay rent with no money?" I inquired.

Erica smacked her lips again. "I'ma ask Eli for a monthly allowance."

I shook my head at how naïve my baby sister was.

"He gives me money anyways so why wouldn't he help me move out?"

"Let me get this straight," I started, realizing Erica still had a lot of growing up to do. "You're looking for a handout all while trying to prove a point to Mama, because it's your prerogative to have sex?" I asked for clarification.

She sighed. "I mean when you say it like that, it sounds stupid."

"*Bingo!*"

"You moved out when you were my age," she shot back. "Eli helped you sometimes too."

"I didn't need Eli's money, though," I clarified. "When I saved up for a car, I quit slaving at McDonald's and started working at the county." I was a correctional officer for six years. "Any time Eli offered to help, I told him no." The only thing I needed Eli for back then was to keep the maintenance up on my car and even then, I didn't have to ask. My brother made sure my whip kept shit like oil changes, tune ups, and fresh tires.

"Why do y'all want me to have this stressful-ass life?" she argued. "I'm sorry I have it easier, but that's not my fault."

I rolled my eyes at her. Erica was missing the point. It wasn't about her having a better life because I wanted that for my sister. We'd suffered enough as kids. Erica was unappreciative. She knew that if all else failed, she could call on me or Eli.

"Erica, just go apologize for screwin' in my Mama's house." It was just that simple.

She scoffed. "She has sex here *all the time*. She don't pay bills. *Eli* does."

I was officially over the conversation. "I'm about to hang up on you."

Erica snickered. "I'm just sayin'."

"No, you just sound stupid."

"Whatever," she mumbled. "Can I move in with you then?"

"So, you can give me grey hairs and send me to an early grave?"

She groaned.

"I don't think so. Stay where you are and go apologize to Mama," I said just as Hakim started calling. I'd forgotten all about him.

"Can you at least think about it?"

"No." I frowned.

"*Please?*" she whined.

My head swayed from side to side. "Nope." Erica had no real reason for wanting to move out. She just wanted more freedom. I was almost positive if Eli found about this condom incident, she wouldn't have a car anymore.

Hakim continued calling.

"*Pretty* please?"

I rolled my eyes.

"I'll get a job."

"You need to be looking for one anyway." I watched Toni play with the toys attached to her swing.

"How do y'all expect me to go to school and work a job?"

"Bye, Erica."

She laughed. "I'll give you a couple days to think it over. Love you!"

"I'm not..." I snatched up my phone when she hung on me. In the middle of me sending her a text, Hakim started calling again. I answered with my eyes trained on Toni. "Hello?" I put the phone on speaker.

"That's how you do me?" He chuckled. "Couldn't even click over and tell a nigga you'd call him back. You got it."

I snickered. "My bad."

"You know how you can make it up to me, right?"

"Nah!" Tone's voice made me freeze and then look at the door. "She don't!"

TONE

I bit down on my bottom lip to keep from cussing Erin out in front my daughter.

I watched her roll her eyes at me and then smack her lips. "Hakim, I'll call you back, okay?"

My mug deepened.

"A'ight, E. I'll be waitin'."

I chuckled.

She hung up the phone and picked up a book that was sitting on the table.

"Who the fuck is Hakim?"

Erin ignored me. She smooth played me off as she opened up a thick book. "Stop cussing in front of Toni." She smirked.

I'm 'bout to choke this bitch.

I chewed down hard on the gum in my mouth.

"And why do you keep coming to my house unannounced?" she asked, still looking down.

My eyes danced around Erin as I contemplated my next move. I was gon' find out who this nigga, Hakim, was.

"How do you keep gettin' a key?" Finally, she looked up at me. "I change the locks and you get a key. I *take* your key and you get another key." She frowned. "You don't live here, Santonio."

I went to Toni and picked her up. I needed to get as far away from my baby mama as possible. I started out of the room, kissing Toni's cheeks repeatedly. She smelled exactly the way Sanaa did when she was this small—like baby powder and milk. Toni yanked on my chains and when she tried to bite down on one, I pulled it out of her tiny grasp. She had a fit after that.

"Stop all that whining." I pecked her chunky cheeks. "Daddy ain't raising no punk, Toni-noni."

She threw her head back and cried.

"I'm sorry." I nuzzled her neck. "Daddy didn't mean to hurt the baby's feelings." We ended up in Erin's room.

Toni was mean like her mama, so my apology didn't matter to her. She snatched my chain again and I let her have it. I sat down with her in the sitting area. I noticed her binky and grabbed it up. I held it in my mouth and put her down on the carpet in front of me.

"Here you go." I handed Toni her Winnie the Pooh pacifier. She gladly took it from me and shoved it in her mouth.

I went into my pocket for my phone, pulled up my contacts and pressed Ava's name.

"What's up?" As usual, she sounded like she had an attitude.

I watched Toni scoot around on her stomach. I chuckled when she rolled over on her side. "Just wanted to make sure you had shit ready for Portland tomorrow."

She yawned. "I'm always ready. But I've been meaning to tell you about them cats out there."

I frowned, placing Toni back on her stomach.

"They're a group of disrespectful-ass niggas."

"Oh, yeah?" I tugged at my beard. "How so?" I wasn't surprised. We always had issues in Portland. Bruce Capporelli and I seemed to bump heads every time he knew I was coming. His father reigned over the cartel and he showed me mad love. Bruce, however, couldn't stand a nigga.

"Yeah. I called that Bruce cat and he spazzed out. Some shit about how he didn't have to take orders from you."

I shook my head.

"I simply told him the orders weren't from you. They were from Don Capporelli. He called me all types of nigger bitches."

I nodded. "I'ma handle that." Once Ava agreed to handle my business affairs, she became *my* responsibility. Yeah, Roman was her man, and I knew he'd protect her, but I couldn't let Bruce get away with talking to her like that. Disrespecting Ava was like disrespecting me, and Bruce knew it.

"A'ight. I'll send the location to everybody at midnight. I got us all up at the Nines. So far, it's Kai Money, Chris, Javier, and Gunz." I heard her shuffling around. "That's all, right?"

"Yeah."

"Okay, cool. Transportation has been handled too."

I nodded. "A'ight, I'll see you in Portland tomorrow afternoon."

"Later."

Hanging up the phone, my eyes landed on Toni again. She was back on her side, babbling loud. She now only had one sock on, exposing her tiny orange toenails. I laughed, reaching over to pick her up.

"When did you start getting your toes done?"

Still sucking on her pacifier, she tugged at my chains.

"You got your own chain to break." I balanced her on my lap. I grabbed the remote next to me and turned the TV on. Then I changed the channel to ESPN.

As I watched highlights from the Chiefs' game, Toni fell asleep on my chest. The only time Toni whined and cried was when she was tired, so I wasn't surprised. I started dozing off too, but the sound of Erin entering her room made me look up at her. With a book in hand, she made her way over to her bed and tossed it down.

"When are you leaving?" She made her way towards me.

"In a minute." I rubbed Toni's back when she started stirring.

"Okay, well put Toni in her bed. I turned on the baby monitor in her room already." Erin spun back around and went to the dresser on the side of her bed.

8

WHEN DO THE TEARS STOP?

ERIN

C utting the water off, I sighed before taking a step out of the shower. I had a busy day ahead of me so I wanted to get to bed early. After wrapping my robe around me, I stood in front of the mirror and took in my reflection. On the outside, it looked like I had everything in order. One would think because of the house I lived in, the clothes I sported, or the cars I drove, I wouldn't have any complaints.

But I did.

I was sad. Depressed, heartbroken, fed up, and confused. I wanted to ball up in a corner and cry my eyes out. I wanted to remove myself from the world and the people around me. Besides Sanaa and Toni, I felt all alone.

Most people looked at me, saw my hard exterior, and assumed I dealt with pain differently. But I didn't. I bled the same as the next person. The only true difference was I pushed on and forced myself to move forward. If my mother taught me anything, it was to be resilient. I didn't depend on people to be there and in all honesty, I expected everybody who claimed to love me to let me down.

That's just the way life was, though.

My hand trembled as I brushed my teeth, so I closed my eyes to recollect myself. I quickly said a silent prayer, asking God to continue to give me wisdom and most importantly strength. When I opened my eyes again, they were misty, but I stuck my chest out and rinsed my mouth. I turned the faucet off and quickly brushed the arm of my cotton robe across my lips. I cut the light out and made my exit. I frowned when I saw Santonio sitting on my bed slumped over with his face in his hands.

He was in nothing but black briefs. I stood there for a minute taking him in. I loved everything about his body. Over the years, he'd been hitting the gym more and it was showing. Santonio wasn't ridiculously buff, but he was well defined. Tattoos were everywhere covering his arms, chest, back, legs, and hands. He even had an "S" for Sanaa next to his right eye and a "T" for Toni on his left. Underneath all that ink was pretty caramel skin.

Swallowing back the curse words to express my irritation, I crossed my arms over my chest.

"I thought you were leaving."

"I am." He still hadn't looked up at me.

"When?"

"After I make love to you." His head rose slowly. Hazel orbs ripped through my soul, forcing me to take a deep breath. "Come here, Erin."

I bit down on my bottom lip, but my feet stayed planted. I didn't want Santonio inside of me. I was already feeling vulnerable. My mental state couldn't handle him caressing me, kissing me, stroking me, holding me or *loving* me.

He pushed off the bed and I involuntarily took a small step back.

"Come here, baby."

I looked away from him and started towards my underwear drawer. Halfway to it, I was swooped up into his big arms. My heart did a somersault.

"Santonio..." I sighed.

He kissed my neck.

"Stop."

He carried me to the bed.

"*Tone...*" I tried to harden my voice, but it didn't work.

Still in his arms, Santonio got on the bed and laid me down. He hovered over me for a moment, just staring at me. I stared back. My eyes were misty again, but this time because I knew no matter what, I would always love this man. I knew he would always hold the key to my heart and I no doubt had the key to his. The mist turned into tears threatening to fall because I knew Santonio didn't deserve me. He knew it too.

It wasn't fair that he could so easily disregard my feelings. It wasn't right that no matter what, he always found himself comfortably in my bed and snug between my legs. But I let him, because I loved him. Finally, we broke eye contact and I stared up at the ceiling. The first tear slid down my cheek and into my ear when he undid my robe and placed a soft kiss on my heart.

"I love you," he whispered as he trailed kisses down my chest, over my stomach and down to my love.

I knew that. I never said he didn't *love* me, but he didn't *deserve* me.

"I'm sorry," he whispered, spreading my legs further part. "I wanna come home, baby." His tongue swirled around my clit.

"Mmm..." My body relaxed. I closed my eyes and widened the gap between my thighs. "*Yes.*"

Santonio's tongue flickered furiously across my nub, making me squirm underneath him. My hips moved, trying to keep up with his pace, but he wrapped his arms around my thighs and locked me down.

"*Santonio...*" I whimpered, feeling my clit swelling.

"Mmm..." he moaned.

"Please don't stop," I begged. "Just like that, baby." My body surrendered to an orgasm as he lapped up all my juices. "Oh my *God.*" My clit throbbed.

Santonio's kisses then trailed back up my body. He leaned over me again and we shared a French kiss. I held on to the sides of his face, tasting myself, but not caring.

"I love you." He broke our kiss to tell me again.

"I know."

Santonio just didn't know *how* to love me. We gazed at each other. My chest rose and fell, waiting on his next move, but he just stared at me. The dismal look in his eyes didn't go unnoticed. We both were hurting, unsure of what we were doing; completely lost in incertitude.

Reaching down, I slid his briefs down, releasing his manhood.

He smiled and I rolled my eyes at his cockiness. The first thrust made me gasp. Wrapping my arms around Santonio, I bit down on my lip and closed my eyes. He slow stroked me and pushed my legs back. His thickness was stretching me out, but I welcomed the pain because it was worth the pleasure.

"*Fuck...*" Santonio whispered into my mouth. His body shuddered, and his eyes got heavy.

Grabbing both sides of his face, I stuck my tongue in his mouth and we shared a deep, passionate kiss. Santonio pushed my legs back and if possible, went deeper. Soft moans escaped my lips as he lifted me a little and wrapped his big arms around me.

"Baby..." I whispered.

"I love you, E." He slid me up and down on the head of his dick. "I love you, baby." The vulnerability in his raspy chords as he looked deep into my eyes and my soul had me on the verge of cumming.

"I love you too." I broke, unable to help it.

"I'ma do better," he promised, grinding deep. "I need you, E." Santonio wrapped his hand around my throat and pulled me closer for a kiss.

"I'm 'bout to cum." I tried to break away from his hold on me. I loved Santonio too much for him to be handling my body like this; like he wouldn't hurt me again and he would do right because he was afraid to lose me.

"Cum for me, baby."

I did. It felt like everything around me was moving in slow motion. I could feel Santonio still moving, but I'd officially checked out. An orgasm ripped through my body, causing my toes to point and my legs to twitch. When Santonio started pounding me, my eyes shut tight and my orgasm heightened.

"Santonio..." I let out a muffled cry.

He pounded harder, digging *deeper*.

"Aaaggghhh fuck!" I screamed. "Baby!" I wrapped my arms around Santonio's neck and held on tight.

"I love you," Tone repeated. "I love you, Ma." His pace picked up.

Our bodies rocked back and forth fervently. When he started cumming, the look on his face wet my pussy up even more. I took that opportunity to gain some sort of control and slow winded my hips, milking him for everything he had. He trembled slightly before letting out a deep yet steady breath. When he came down from his orgasmic high, we indulged in another heartfelt kiss.

Santonio broke our lip lock and began fondling my breasts. I chewed on my bottom lip as his tongue snaked around my erect nipples. Closing my eyes, I enjoyed the warmness of his mouth and his gentle but firm touch. He caressed my thigh with one hand as he reached up and gripped my neck again with the other. His tongue then slithered up my chest and he planted another kiss on my heart.

When he got to my neck, he sucked hard putting a hickey on my neck. I rested my head back basking in the feel of him. He then placed soft kisses up my neck, on my chin, and on my lips again. We gazed into each other's eyes for a moment, lost in one another. Santonio's manhood started swelling inside of me again, letting me know it was going to be a long night.

TONE

Resting back in my chair, I watched niggas take their seats around the table. On the left of me sat Kai Money, a heavy hitter. Other than my guys in Kansas City, Kai Money was one of the only cats I trusted with my life. He lived in New York, but he was born and bred in Kansas City. He'd done time in the pen on a murder and gun charge, but after a short conversation with the judge, I got his sentence cut more than half.

Gunz was outside in the car with Javier, and Chris was back at the hotel with Ava. I tugged at my beard and waited for Don Capporelli to come in and take his seat at the table. Bruce entered with two cats walking next to him as his bodyguards. I kept my eyes trained on him, and when he took a seat, he looked to me and smirked. The cat to the right of him placed his gun down on the table and stared between Kai Money and me.

"Yo, this nigga got beef?" Kai went to his side for his piece and placed it on the table as well.

Bruce chuckled. "Santonio, it's good to see you. I've been looking forward to this reunion." His Italian accent made his English sound broken.

I stared back at him. "You owe my business partner an apology."

"*Ava*, right?"

Kai tensed next to me. He and Ava were like brother and sister.

"That's right. But since she's not here, you can run it by me and I'll deliver it for you." I smirked.

Bruce mugged me. "Over my dead body."

"Bet." Kai nodded.

"You threat—"

Bruce was cut short when the big double doors to the room swung open.

"Gentlemen..." Don Capporelli clasped his hands together and then gazed around the room. "Familia..." He smiled. "It's been a long time since I've had the opportunity to have you all here at once."

Don Capporelli stepped further into the room. "Bruce, Maine, Carter, and Santonio..." His eyes landed on me. "I'll need to speak with you separately." He took a seat at the head of the table in a gold trimmed chair that was made to look like a throne.

When he flipped his right hand that was blinged out in gold rings, the men at the table simultaneously got up. Kai Money rose from his seat with his eyes still trained on Bruce before he made his exit.

"I'm sensing some hostility, no?" Don Capporelli sounded amused.

I stayed quiet. However, Bruce started whining like the bitch he was.

"Can we discuss respect?"

Don Capporelli waited on him to continue, twisting the ring on his pinky finger.

"When I go to Arizona, I have the decency to contact Maine, and when I go to Virginia, I reach out to Carter."

Don Capporelli looked to me quickly and then back to his son.

"They both show me the same respect. They don't just come to my city and make themselves at home," he spat and then started rambling on in his native tongue.

I chuckled. Bruce was a spoiled bitch. I hadn't left the comfort of Erin's bed to deal with this shit. If I wanted to argue on some punk shit, then I would've stayed at home with her.

Don Capporelli held his hand up silencing Bruce. He then looked to me. "Santonio, what seems to be the issue?" He put a cigar in his mouth and his bodyguard lit it.

"Issue?" I looked to Bruce. "I didn't know it was an issue."

Bruce slammed his hand down on the table. "This nigger has no respect for me. I am a Capporelli. He should be praising me. Thanking his Muslim God for his seat at *my* table."

"Fuck you, Guido." I flexed.

"*Sta 'zitto!*" Don Capporelli yelled. "Both of you." He sighed.

"Father, he must learn to—"

Don held his hand up again. "The Masseria family will be here tomorrow. You will not embarrass the Capporelli name." He glared at Bruce. "Whatever disagreements you may have will be left in this room at this table. If you humiliate me..." His eyes bounced back and forth between Bruce and me. "Tiucciderò, mi haicapito?"

I nodded, fully understanding that Don, had just threatened to kill us.

Bruce sucked his teeth. "Se posso, signore, francamente... penso che stia dando troppo potere a questo bambino." He rambled.

"I'm a grown-ass man," I said, grilling him. "Any power Don Capporelli gave me, I earned the shit. Take that up with *him* and not me." I understood Italian well. He could've just said the shit in English. He was pressed about my rank in the Capporelli family, calling me a kid and saying Don Capporelli gave me too much power.

Bruce scoffed.

"I've said what I had to say." Don Capporelli nodded towards the door and his bodyguard went to open it to let everyone back in. "Ah, yes, Figlio," he spoke to Bruce, puffing hard on his Cuban cigar. "I believe you owe Ms. Lane an apology."

9

KILL 'EM WITH KINDNESS. ANGER IS A WEAKNESS

ERIN

"**D**o you think I'm a push over?" Chance sat next to me while we got pedicures.

I looked down at the fingernail polish in my hand. I was having a hard time picking a color. "Sometimes." I shrugged.

She sighed.

"Why? What happened?" I decided on a light pink.

"I'm really getting tired of that Nisha chick and Chasity's mama," she pouted. "True made her get an abortion and she's been on Facebook dragging my name through the mud."

I shook my head, relaxing in my seat. "Saying what?" Chance was loyal to True, so she dealt with a lot of bullshit that she didn't have to. I still questioned her and True's friendship. Supposedly, they hadn't fucked, but she was super close to his kids and his family. Besides her donut shop, thanks to True, she hadn't worked a day in her life.

"Saying I'm not a *real* woman because I didn't try to convince True not to make her do it. Like I told True, if you don't want any kids by her, then wear a damn condom or get her some birth control." She stared down at the yellow polish in her hand. "It's not rocket science."

"Didn't Ava already check her?"

Chance nodded. "Twice. Ava swears if she has to say anything else to Nisha, she's going to tase her."

I chuckled. Ava's ass was wild.

"We shouldn't have to resort to violence just to get a point across."

"Bitches like Nisha don't see it that way," I told her honestly. I agreed with Chance. Violence wasn't always the key. However, Chance was also best friends with one of the biggest bullies and killers on Tone's team.

"Well, I just want her to leave me alone."

"What did True say?"

"He told me not to let her see me sweat."

"I like that advice."

Chance was sensitive and timid as hell. She let what others thought of her dictate how she lived her life. So, what if Nisha or Chasity's mama didn't like her? They only hated Chance because she had something they'd never get: True's heart.

Chance's phone went off and she smacked her lips. "Hello?"

I searched for a new book to download on my Kindle app.

"I'm not, True." Chance sighed. "I'm with Erin getting a pedicure."

A text alert from Santonio flashed across the screen.

BD: Come fly out to Portland. I miss you

I rolled my eyes.

Me: Just because we had sex doesn't mean I like you.

I continued my search for a good book.

"True, then you should stop messing with her if you don't see a future with the girl," Chance snapped in a hushed tone. "Why are you playing with her feelings? I might not like her, but that's not fair."

BD: Where Toni and Sanaa at?

Me: With my mom.

The bell at the shop's door rang and I looked up to see Sasha coming in. I wasn't surprised to see her. We'd been coming to the same nail tech for two years now. She scanned the room and when her eyes landed on me, she rolled them. I frowned and was getting ready to speak when my phone started ringing.

"What's up, Hakim?"

"Shit, you tell me." He chuckled. "I'ma be back in Missouri in two days. You gon' let me take you out?"

I smiled. Hakim wouldn't let up on spending time with me. If he wasn't texting, he was calling, and if we were both just chilling, he'd FaceTime me.

"If I'm not busy, yes, we can go out."

"I'll be there Friday night. Don't make plans Saturday. I want you all to myself."

"And what if I can't find a baby sitter?" Nine times out of ten, the girls would be with their daddy, but who said I wanted to give Hakim my whole day?

He chuckled. "Then I'll find something kid-friendly to do and you can bring them too."

Santonio would have a fit if I brought another man around our daughters. I wouldn't even disrespect him like that.

"I'll see if I can fit you in." I smiled again, knowing he wasn't going to give up.

"I'll see you Saturday, E. Stay safe." And with that he hung up.

When I looked over at Chance, she was already staring at me. "What?"

"You haven't learned, I see." She sighed.

I laughed. "Chance, I can't put my life on pause because my baby daddy is a nut." Hakim and I were cool way before I knew Santonio even existed.

"Okay..." She gave me a look. "What you think about this yellow?" she asked, holding it up so I could see. "I know it's out of season, but I need some color in my life."

"I like it."

She nodded and then cleared her throat. "Hey, Sasha. I haven't seen you in a minute, girl." Chance looked at me.

I rolled my eyes before giving my attention back to my phone.

"I've just been staying in my own lane," she said smartly.

"Oh... Okay."

An awkward silence fell over the shop. And then...

"Y'all missing somebody, ain't y'all?" Sasha stated, sorting through gel colors.

I looked up at her.

"What's her name? *Ava?* Where she at? Somewhere suckin' dick?" *What the hell, Sasha?*

Whatever she and Eli were going through had her acting out of character.

Chance sighed. "Ava is out of town and Roman's not with her." The irritation in her tone made me look over at her. Chance was glaring at Sasha. "Whatever problem you have with Ava should probably be addressed with Eli."

"Whatever."

I counted back from five. "Yo, Sash, what's up wit' you?"

"Erin, stop talking to me. You said everything you had to say at my house."

The Asian woman doing my feet was about to start polishing my toenails, but I held my hand up to stop her.

"Erin..." Chance groaned lowly.

I ignored her and stood up. Making my way over to Sasha, I crossed my arms over my chest. "You're really beefing over this stupid shit? None of this shit has anything to do with me."

Sasha pushed her chair back and stood up. "This has *everything* to do with you, Erin."

"Y'all..." I didn't even notice Chance had stood from her seat. "Let's not do this here."

"Chance, mind your business," Sasha snapped, staring at me. "Erin, how long have I known you? A long time, right?" she answered for me.

I was now confused.

"Instead of talking to your brother, telling him he had a good woman at home, you condoned him fuckin' off on me."

"What?!" I shouted. I didn't condone cheating. I despised the shit.

Sasha smacked her lips. "So, Yvonne didn't come to your house to see Eli?" she asked, referring to Eli's first baby mama.

"Okay?" Yvonne only came over to get money from him. My mama didn't like her, so she wasn't allowed to come to her house. And she and Sasha couldn't stand each other, so Eli kept them apart. Sasha was my girl and all, but I wasn't obligated to report back to her whenever a bitch was in Eli's face.

Sasha mugged me. "You ain't no real friend, because if you were, you would've called and told me."

Okay, so the bitch is delusional.

"Please take a seat or I'm going to have to ask you to leave."

I ignored Henry, the nail tech, and stepped closer to Sasha. "Called and told you what? That Eli's baby mama came to get money from him for *his* son? If you weren't so damn insecure, he probably would've had her come to y'all's house to get it." Sasha was blowing my high. Where was all this animosity coming from?

"Yeah, but they fucked in your bathroom. You gon' act like you didn't know that?"

I threw my hands up and walked away. Hell no, I didn't know Eli had screwed Yvonne in my house. I would've cussed both of their asses out. When Yvonne pulled up, I was leaving to go take my ladybugs to their doctor's appointment. I stayed around long enough to see him cash her out and tell Yvonne to bring my nephew over.

Eli knew where the spare key to my house was, so I trusted him to lock up after he left. *This* was why I didn't want my friends fucking my brother. I wasn't about to change the dynamic of my relationship with Eli for *nobody*. Sasha expected me to choose a side and I wasn't going to do that. After retaking my seat at the pedicure bowl, I pulled up my Kindle app and continued my search for a fire read.

Chance got to her chair, snatched up her shoes and purse, and slid her feet into her Nike slides. "I'll talk to you later, Erin." She stormed towards the exit.

Great. Now I'ma have to hear True's mouth.

TONE

I sat at a round table decorated with a red linen table cloth. A gold ice bucket chilling a bottle of champagne was the center piece. A gold name plate sat next to the bucket with "Santonio" engraved on it since the table was reserved for me and my team. The chairs were plush enough to make me feel like I was sitting on cotton and the Henny in my cup had me wishing I was at home. The ballroom was full of people, but I was in my own zone. Italian dance music seeped from the speakers even though the crowd was a mix of different races.

Only two people were still seated at the table with me. Kai Money had excused himself to go call his wife, and Chris was on the hunt for pussy. Ava sat two chairs away from me in her navy-blue gown, sipping from a champagne flute, and Gunz was next to her. Taking another drink from my glass, I scanned the room again. The Capporelli and Masseria families appeared to be mingling well. I wasn't into making new relationships, so I played the background.

When I noticed Don Capporelli approaching me with District Attorney Ralph Esposito, I sat my drink down and fixed the sleeves on my suit jacket. I knocked twice on the table, gaining Ava's attention. She put her flute down, sat up in her seat, and smoothed the front of her dress down. Gunz got up from his seat and walked away. I stood up and waited for both men to reach my table.

"Santonio..." Don Capporelli smiled. "You know Ralph, no?"

I nodded. "Yeah, I know Mr. Esposito."

Ralph held his hand out for a handshake. "It's good to see you again."

"Likewise." I glanced at Ava and she rose from her seat. "This is Ava Lane."

She smiled giving a small nod.

Ralph's eyes lit up. "Beautiful. Very beautiful and *radiant*..." He licked his lips.

I chuckled. The smile on Ava's face had long since vanished.

"Gentlemen." She gave another small head nod.

Don Capporelli's smile widened. "Esposito, Ms. Lane is one of few ladies in the Capporelli family. She's well respected, dedicated, and rather feisty." He gave a hearty laugh and District Attorney Esposito joined in.

My eyes bounced to Ava who looked like she'd rather be some-where else.

"She's very pretty too." DA Esposito licked his lips.

"And taken," she announced smugly with her head tilted slightly.

Don Capporelli chuckled. "I was just telling Esposito about your expansion." He tapped me lightly on the back. "Santonio reminds me of me when I was younger. Molto fedele...very loyal."

"I've crossed path with Mr. Morris." Esposito stared at me.

Don Capporelli nodded.

From my peripheral, I could see Bruce and one other cat heading in our direction. I looked to Ava and she excused herself from the table. I adjusted my jacket once more as they approached us.

"Father." Bruce took a stand next to Don Capporelli. He was drunk as fuck, barely able to stand, dude was swaying and shit. "I want you to meet Hakim," he slurred.

My eyes shot in ole boy's direction.

Hakim...

Don Capporelli took a step away from him. "I'm busy right now. That can wait, no?"

Bruce frowned. "Busy doing what? I don't see you talking to anyone important."

Don Capporelli stared at him.

"You seem to like this *boy* from Kansas City so much." He glared at me. "Hakim was born and raised there too."

Oh yeah?

I tugged at my beard. Erin had me fucked up. I wasn't sure if this was the Hakim she'd been on the phone with or not, but I was going to get down to the bottom of it. If this was the same nigga, then she was fucking with the help. And if either one of them thought I was going to let it ride, they were both in for a deadly awakening.

Don Capporelli twisted his pinky ring. "I've asked you to be respectful, but you have disregarded my request," he spoke to Bruce, but kept his eyes on Hakim.

"Fa-"

"Mostraunpo' di rispetto per tuo padre!"

Bruce quickly stumbled away with Hakim following him.

"Esposito, come, I want you to meet Xenia Masseria. She'll be working close with Santonio." Don Capporelli tapped my arm once more before he took off.

When they walked away, I watched Bruce and Hakim as they exchanged words by the refreshment table. Being in the game for so long had heightened my senses, so I always trusted my gut instinct. I'd already known for a while that Bruce couldn't be trusted and neither could the company he kept. I was sure that the only reason Don Capporelli hadn't killed him by now was because they were family. But something was off and I could feel it strongly. A storm was brewing. My assumption was confirmed when Hakim looked in my direction and smirked.

10

YOU ONLY WANT ME WHEN I'M NOT THERE.

ERIN

"I'm glad I'm finally getting a chance to sit down with you." My mom glanced up from her menu to look at me.

We were having brunch as an attempt to catch up since we hadn't spoken in almost a week.

"I know."

"Eli told me you and Sasha had a falling out. What's going on?" She picked up her wineglass.

I shrugged. "She and Eli are going through some things and she's taking it on everybody else except him."

She nodded. "I don't even know why that girl started messing with him in the first place."

I stared down at my menu.

"So, what's new?" she asked before taking another sip of wine.

"Nothing for real."

"Mmm, how are things between you and Santonio?"

"Same ole."

She smacked her lips. "Erin, is there a reason you're being short with me?"

I picked up my wineglass. "You asked me a question and I gave you an answer."

"You're grown, but I'm still your mama, so lower your tone and fix your face."

"Ma, I'm tired and I don't feel like being interrogated."

"Girl, please. I'm not interrogating you. I'm taking interest in your life. I don't see or talk to you as much as I do Eli and Erica." She sat her glass down and picked her phone up. "I'm just worried about you. That's all."

"No need to worry. I'm good." I downed as much wine as I could without choking. Lately, I hadn't been feeling comfortable opening up to anybody about the things I was going through. People put on fronts and pretended to care when in actuality nobody really gave a fuck.

"Your grandparents are coming to visit for Thanksgiving. Mama still hasn't met Toni, so you know she's mad at you." She chuckled.

"She has my number."

My mom shook her head at me. "And you have hers."

"I'll reach out," I mumbled.

"Today?"

"Ma—"

"Today, Erin! Your grandma misses you."

I nodded.

"Did your sister tell you she's trying to convince me to let her move out?"

I nodded again.

"Ever since she started having sex, Erica's been real disrespectful. I told her if she keeps it up, I'm telling Eli and I'll let him deal with her."

"She asked me if she could move in with me."

My mama sucked her teeth. "Take her. I can't deal with her too much longer; at least for the school year." She looked up at the waiter when he approached the table and smiled. "Can you give us a little while longer?"

"Take your time." He smiled back before walking off.

"Do you really think Erica moving in with me will change her attitude?" I didn't. Erica was in her selfish phase. We'd all been there. My little sister was just spoiled on top of everything else.

"I don't know. But you have that big house with just you and my grandbabies. With her being there, it'll give you some freedom and a break from being a mommy every once in a while."

I chuckled. My mother was really trying to pawn my sister off on me.

She laughed, picking up her wine glass. "I'm serious. Mama needs a break. I told your granddad when Erica graduates, I'm going to travel for a year." She took a sip of wine. "I've already applied for my passport."

I only shook my head at my mama.

"I might even move out of state and find me a fine man that'll cater to my needs." She smirked.

"Really, Ma?" I laughed. "You could've kept that to yourself."

She waved me off. "You have two kids. You know all about good dick."

Oh my God...

She eyed me suspiciously. "Speaking of good dick, are you still screwing Santonio?"

"Aren't you supposed to be deciding what you want to eat?" I picked my menu again.

"That's a yes." She finished off her wine. "I thought you were going to start dating."

"I am."

"Then why are you still entertaining Santonio? I swear between him and TreVell, I don't know who's worse."

Hearing TreVell's name brought back memories of my late teens to early twenties. He was my first real boyfriend. We'd lived together for years and then all of sudden, things between us changed. Just like Santonio, he was a womanizer. The only difference was TreVell took his cheating to a whole other level.

He'd stay gone for days and then lie, saying he'd been in jail. He'd let bitches drive my car around while I was at work and then fuck them in the home we shared in the bed where I laid my head. I lost count of all the times some mad hoe had put my car in the shop from doing stupid shit like breaking my windows, flattening my tires, or putting sugar in my tank. At least Santonio kept his bitches in check. So far, I only knew about one—Amina. And that was because she and Jeanette had been cool.

I hadn't spoken to TreVell since Nette's funeral. His mother wrote me on Facebook a little while ago and asked had a talked to him, but I hadn't. She claimed he had left her a message saying he was moving out of town and hadn't heard from him since. At first, I was a little thrown off by that since he was a mama's boy, but with TreVell you just never knew what he was capable of. I hoped he was okay, though. I didn't wish harm on anyone.

"Santonio knows we're done."

"Then why do you keep letting him in your bed?"

"Ma!" She had some nerve. She snuck around with my father for years behind his wife's back.

"I'm just saying, Erin." Her left eyebrow rose.

"Ma, Santonio is nothing more than the father of my kids."

She smacked her lips. "You said that after you had Sanaa. And then came Toni."

I massaged my temples.

"All that money doesn't overshadow the fact that he has a lot of growing up to do." She frowned.

"You ladies ready to order?" The waiter was back at our table.

"I'm fine. You mind bringing the whole bottle of wine out?" I downed the rest of my drink.

"Erin, you need to eat."

I ignored her.

"Okay..." She sighed. My mom then ran her order off and the waiter jotted it down before walking off again. "So, now you have an attitude."

"I don't."

"You know you're too old to be throwing hissy fits. Then you have the nerve to wonder why Sanaa is such a diva." She stared at me.

"Did we come here to talk about Santonio?"

She shook her head disapprovingly. "You're not going to learn until you end up pregnant *again*. Tone has you right where he wants you."

She kept on rambling and a text from Hakim flashed across my screen.

Hakim: *I'll pick you up tomorrow at 4.*

Me: *I'll meet you. Text me the info.*

TONE

I let myself in my Ma Duke's crib and made my way towards the kitchen. When I entered, Sanaa was sitting at the table with Rajon eating pizza.

"Hi, Daddy." She cheesed, trying to wipe her hands with a napkin.

"Sup, Naa-Naa?" I approached her and placed a kiss on her forehead.

"'Sup, Uncle Tone?" Rajon said with a full mouth.

I gave him a quick pound. "What's goin' on, nephew?"

I went to the counter, opened the Pizza Hut box and removed a slice of pepperoni pizza. Leaning against the counter, I quickly demolished the slice as Sanaa and Rajon argued about her not being able to dribble a basketball. The patio door opened and my Aunt Paige stepped in. She was Ma Dukes baby sister and my least favorite auntie. She was also Deidra's mama. Aunt Paige thought she was better than everybody and always had her fuckin' nose in the air.

"Hey, Santonio. When did you get here?" She trekked towards the refrigerator.

I shrugged. "A lil' while ago."

"Good," she said, opening the door. "Toni's out there with the worst attitude like her mama."

Aunt Paige would never say it, but she didn't like Erin. It was most likely because of Skyy, Erin's best friend, and my uncle Derick's affair. Even though neither E nor Skyy knew he was married, my auntie was still holding a grudge.

"Not too much on my loves." I wiped my hands down with a paper towel and started towards the patio.

"Daddy, can I go wit' you?" Sanaa asked, making me stop to look at her.

"I'm not going nowhere, Naa."

"She talkin' 'bout if you do," Rajon said, balling up a napkin and then attempting a shot at the trashcan. He missed and then sucked his teeth.

Stepping outside, I was welcomed by the sounds of laughter and the foul smell of cigarette smoke. Ma Duke had Toni in her lap and Aunt Macie was standing off to the side with my Aunt Daisy.

"Oh, hey, baby." Ma Duke smiled at me, bouncing Toni.

"Sup, Ma?" I held out my arms for Toni. My baby damn near jumped out of moms' arms to get to me.

"What y'all out here gossiping about?" I kissed Toni's cheek and she grabbed for my chains.

"We're deciding if we're going two stepping or not."

I nodded.

"You can't speak?" Aunt Daisy slurred, approaching us. "Just because you're grown don't mean I won't kick your ass," she threatened playfully as I pulled her into a side hug.

I chuckled. "Sup, Auntie? What you out here drinkin'?"

"Don't worry about all that." She hit my arm. "Let your auntie hold something," she asked and Ma Duke smacked her lips.

I went into my pocket, pulled out a roll of cash, and passed it to her. "Take what you need." I kissed Toni again and took a seat.

"You ain't doing nothing but supporting her drinking habit." Ma Duke snatched the roll out of Aunt Daisy's hand, unraveled it, and peeled off a few bills.

"Oh, sister..." She laughed. "Don't be acting like that." Aunt Daisy took the money and stuffed it into her bra. "Thank you, nephew." She staggered to a vacant seat and dropped down.

"I don't know why Sadee's acting like that. She don't want the boys giving nobody money but her."

I knew Aunt Macie was about to start. For some reason, she couldn't stand Ma Duke. What I didn't understand was why Ma Duke had raised my cousin, Roman, for her. They had some unspoken beef and they'd been constantly bumping heads lately.

Ma Duke sighed. "Macie, not today. I haven't seen Daisy in weeks and I just want to relax with my sisters."

"I'm just saying. You think you sit on this imaginary throne, but you don't."

I frowned.

"Macie, why are you always so mad?" Aunt Daisy stood up. "Let me go check on the kids."

"What's going on out here?" Aunt Paige's ghetto ass bopped out onto the patio.

Ma Duke reached over to fix the cuff in Toni's jeans. "Nothing."

"Sadee being Sadee," Aunt Macie said with an attitude. "She thinks she runs everything and damn everybody."

"Watch your mouth." I glared at her. "If being around my mom is so hard, quit coming over here."

Ma Duke tapped my arm. "Stop, Santonio. You're only making it worse."

I shook her hand off me. "Nah, she can bounce."

"Shit!" Macie snatched up her purse. "You ain't gotta tell me twice."

Aunt Paige smacked her lips. "No, Macie, sit down."

"For what? So, I can continue to be disrespected?" Macie's eyes landed on me. "You over here being your mama's Superman while she babysitting so your baby mama can go fuck another man," she spat before storming into the house.

I looked to my moms. "The fuck is she talkin' 'bout?"

"That's my cue to go." Aunt Paige snickered, following her sister.

"Watch your mouth in front of Toni." Ma Duke reminded me.

"Nah, this *my* daughter, so I'ma talk how I want around her." I rose from my seat. "Is Erin out on a date?"

Ma Duke couldn't even look at me.

"Ain't that some shit?" I chuckled, heading for the door. "You out here helping her be a whore." I stepped inside the kitchen. "That's fucked up." I went searching for Sanaa since she wasn't at the table eating anymore.

"Tonio, I didn't know she was going on a date until I called her to bring Toni some more baby food." Ma Duke followed me through her crib. "She was all dressed up when she came back and told us all she was going out with a friend."

I found Sanaa in the playroom, trying to put a puzzle together. "Naa-Naa, let's roll, baby," I called out to her and she hopped up with a smile.

"So, you're taking them because you're upset with me?"

I ignored Ma Duke as I took Sanaa's small hand into mine and headed for the front door.

"Daddy, Granny talkin' to you," Sanaa said softly.

I gently rubbed my thumb across the back of her hand and ignored her too.

"Santonio Keith Morris, I know you hear me talking to you." Ma Duke followed me.

When we finally reached the front door, she was still on my heels.

"I'll be back to get their bags." I let go of Sanaa's hand and leaned over to pick up Toni's car seat.

"Tonio, you're overreacting."

I kept my mouth closed so I wouldn't disrespect my OG. Opening the door, I let Sanaa walk out first, reminding her to watch her step. We made it to my ride and I opened the back door with my moms still yapping. After placing Toni in her seat, I buckled her in, closed the door, and picked Sanaa up.

"I told you Erin wouldn't wait on you forever," she pressed.

I walked to the driver's side, opened the back door and put Sanaa in. After making sure he seatbelt was secure, I hopped in the front and drove off. I pulled up on a stop sign and called Veronica.

"Daddy, you mad?" Sanaa asked innocently.

"No, Naa, Daddy ain't mad."

Veronica answered the same time a call from Roman beeped in on the other line. I clicked over.

"Wassup?"

"You know BM out here wildin', right?"

I frowned. "Oh, yeah? Where she at?"

"That Mexican restaurant off state-line. The lil' homies just called me. I'm over that way. You want me to go get her?"

I busted an illegal U-turn and headed toward the restaurant. "Nah, but meet me up there." I ended the call.

When I pulled into the parking lot, Roman was sitting on the hood of his whip smoking a blunt. True sat in the passenger's seat on the phone with the door open. I parked next to them and hopped out with my burner.

"Take them to the house for me." I nodded towards my whip.

"A'ight." Roman got down and tucked his gun. "The keys are in the ignition." He told me as I passed by his ride.

Stalking towards the entrance, I cocked my piece and put my finger on the trigger. I swung the door open and the people waiting to be seated jumped up and rushed out.

"Table for one, sir?"

I pushed the hostess out of my way and scanned the room. When my eyes landed on Erin cheesing all hard in some nigga's face, I stormed in her direction.

"Get up."

She looked up at me. The bitch had the nerve to look spooked. Her mouth dropped a little. Her date turned around and I came face to face with that nigga Hakim from Portland. I cracked him hard over the head and he went tumbling over. I spun my gun around and pistol whipped his bitch ass with the handle.

Erin hopped up out of her chair as people scurried around us. *"Santonio!"* she screamed, trying to pull me back by my shirt. "Stop!"

I shoved her away roughly.

"Bro!" True pulled me back. "Come on, blood. Not here." He pushed me towards the exit.

My eyes were in slits as I stared at Hakim's bloody face and head. He was slumped over in the booth looking lifeless. They then darted towards Erin who was yelling, trying to get me to calm down. Once we got outside, it felt like everything started moving in slow motion. I could see True's mouth moving, but I couldn't hear shit the nigga was saying.

I snatched away from True and yanked Erin by her arm. The bitch was dressed like she was about to go clubbing or some shit in a tight-ass, long-sleeve, nude dress and gold heels. I pulled her towards the passenger's side of Roman's ride. True rushed back out of the restaurant carrying Erin's purse just as I shut her door. I hopped in the driver's seat, he jumped in the back, and I peeled out of the parking lot.

11

GOD KNOWS WE TRIED…

ERIN

What if he killed him?

    I couldn't believe Santonio. I sat quietly as he sped down the street. His knuckles were turning white from him gripping the steering wheel so tight. True passed me my purse and I reached in it for my phone. My hands shook as I pulled up my call log to try and call Hakim.

I was hoping someone had his phone. I put the phone to my ear and surprisingly, someone picked up on his end.

"Hello? I don't know this young man, but whoever you are, he's been hurt." The stranger sounded like an elderly woman.

"Has anyone called the ambulance for…"

Santonio snatched my phone out of my hand and tossed it out his window.

"What the fuck is wrong with you!?" I yelled, pushing him. The car swerved a little.

"Aye, E, relax," True spoke from the back seat. "Let him calm down, shorty."

"Fuck you, True!" I screamed, punching Tone. "I hate you! Why the fuck did you do that to him!" I started crying.

Not for Hakim, but for my crazy-ass baby daddy. If Hakim was dead, there were a whole lot of witnesses to tie Santonio to it. That meant Sanaa and Toni wouldn't have their father. Ms. Sadee would be hurt. And *me*, I would...

I punched him harder and in return he shoved me into the door. My head hit the window hard.

"You crying over this nigga?!" Santonio hollered and I flinched a little. "Huh?!"

I cried, wiping the blood from my lip. "Let me out!"

"Man..." True drawled. "Y'all hot."

"Let me out, Santonio!" I cried harder. Tone was going to prison. He'd killed Hakim in front of all those people and they were going to lock him up.

"Shut the fuck up!" He roared back. "Your ass is out here embarrassing a nigga by fuckin' *the help*!"

What?

"I should've murked that nigga." He punched the steering wheel.

"Let me out the car." I sniffled. Red stains were now covering my brand new dress.

"Shut up," he told me firmly. "I should put my foot up yo ass."

Santonio came to a crazy stop in front of my house and got out the car with it still running. I sniffled, watching him making his way around the front of the car and to my side like a raging bull. He yanked my door open and snatched me out of the car. My head flew back and an instant pain shot through back.

"Tone, chill, dawg. Don't do some shit you gon' regret," True tried to reason with him.

"Let me go!" I punched him continuously as he picked me up and tossed me over his shoulder. "Put me down!"

"Yeah..." True said to someone on the phone. "Auntie is already on her way? Cool."

Santonio carried me all the way to the door and when we got to it, the psycho kicked it. The first time I could only hear the frame crack.

The second kick sent the door flying open and crashing off the hinges. I'd never seen him act like this. Even though Santonio had never put his hands on me, I was scared. He then started up the stairs not saying a word.

We reached my room and when we got to my bed he tossed me on it. He paced the floor quietly. I cried with my face in my pillow. I now had a terrible headache and the right side of my face was sore from when I hit the window. I jumped when I heard a loud thud.

Looking up and over at Santonio, I saw he had punched a hole in the wall. He punched two more holes before he took off out of my room. I stayed in the bed, crying softly with my face still deep my pillow. Santonio was really tripping. He was acting like he had caught me fucking Hakim instead of sharing a meal.

The door slammed and through my blurred vision, I watched Santonio approach me. I lay still as he unbuckled and removed my stilettos. He then pulled my dress over my head and slid my panties off. He got up from the bed and stalked towards the bathroom. I heard the shower come on and then a few seconds later, he came back out naked. Scooping me up in his big arms, he carried me to the shower. After sitting me down on the marble shower bench, he stepped back out and went to the sink.

Santonio returned to the shower and handed me a glass of water. I took it and the two Tylenol pills he placed in my palm. I tossed the pills in my mouth and took a long drink of water before giving him the glass back. With my head low, I swallowed my tears. Santonio closed the glass door.

He then picked me up, sat down, and placed me on his lap. Face to face, we stared at one another. The second shower head came on and Santonio broke our gaze and rested his head against the wall. I wrapped my arms around his torso and leaned into his body. Unable to hold back my tears any longer, I cried into his chest.

"I'm sorry," he whispered.

I held on to him tighter.

"I shouldn't have pushed you at the restaurant or in the car." He wrapped his arms around me. "Stop crying, baby."

I couldn't.

"You know I would never hurt you intentionally, right?"

I sniffled.

"I love you, E. This shit is becoming unhealthy for both of us." He sighed. "But I can't let you go. I can't sit back and watch you love another nigga."

I would *never* love another. Tone knew that. But I couldn't keep allowing him to lie and cheat on me. How could I teach my daughters the value of self-respect when their daddy didn't respect their mama? Santonio's and my relationship had become too toxic.

I'd never hit him and he'd never put his hands on me. I cried like a baby thinking about what it would mean if I were to *really* let him go or if he would let *me* go. There would be no more hugs, kisses, laughs, or long conversations. We wouldn't have a future or be a family. No more us.

He sat up straight and hugged me tighter.

None of that mattered if he didn't want to be committed to me, though. I didn't want to share him and I shouldn't have to. It was bad enough he'd lied to me about being so deep in the mob. Santonio had a lot of power; the kind you only saw in movies.

When I found out, he swore the only reason why he'd lied was to keep me safe. So, on top of him living a fast life, I had to raise his two daughters and deal with his constant deceit? Letting Santonio get away with so much had made me his doormat. And because of that, it didn't matter that we loved each other. We couldn't continue to go on like this.

TONE

E's body trembled softly as I stood up with her still in my arms. I was fuckin' up big time. I'd hurt the most important person in my life. Erin hadn't done anything but shown me how down she was. My baby was the true definition of a rider and I'd let her down.

Kissing her neck, I whispered I was sorry again even though I knew it wouldn't change nothing. E was finished. She'd done everything in her power to keep us together. I, on the other hand, had done everything to push her away.

Sliding her down on my dick slowly, I sucked hard on her neck. Standing underneath the shower heads, I stroked her tenderly. I wanted E to *feel* how sorry a nigga was for all my constant lying and cheating. I'd never been good with words so I prayed my baby felt my apology. Sex would never fix her broken heart, but deep down in mine, we both knew nobody could make her feel like I did.

She moaned my name softly as I gripped her ass cheeks and went as deep as she would allow me. Hitting that spot over and over again, I pulled her bottom lip into my mouth and sucked on it.

"I love you."

She moaned.

"I don't wanna let you go." But I had to. We needed to be apart for a little while.

I stopped stroking her and we held on to each other tight. Water cascaded over our heads and trickled down our joined bodies. With her face in my neck, Erin's body bounced lightly as she cried. If it wasn't for the water beating down on us, she would've seen my teary eyes. I loved the fuck out of E, but I'd done this to us.

From this point forward, I could only try to prove that she was my world. My words didn't mean shit to her no more. I was disappointed in myself because Erin had given me so many free passes and I'd dropped the ball every time. Now, I'd probably lost her for good. I hugged her tighter.

"I'm sorry," she whispered.

I frowned. "For what?"

"Not being good enough."

What?

"No matter what I did, it wasn't enough to keep you." She sniffled.

Closing my eyes, I sighed. "E, you are more than enough, baby. You didn't do nothing wrong. This is my fuck up. You're perfect."

She sniffled.

"You gave me two of the greatest gifts a man could ask for. You stuck by a nigga even when you felt deep down I didn't deserve your loyalty."

Erin hugged my neck.

"I want you to learn from me...from *us*." I opened my eyes and a single tear slid down my left cheek. "Ain't no nigga worth crying over, E. You're too good of a woman to have to settle, baby."

Her body relaxed.

"You hear me?"

She nodded and I took a seat on the shower bench.

Bodies still locked and with my dick still inside of her, we clung to each other. I wanted my family, but I wanted peace more than anything for Erin. I wasn't giving up, but I knew we needed some distance. She stopped crying and rested her head on my shoulder. I laid my head back against the shower wall and closed my eyes. We stayed that way until the water got cold.

12

THEY DON'T LOVE YOU LIKE I LOVE YOU

ERIN

"What you back here doin'?" Eli stood at my patio door.

"Basking in the scenery." I stared at my pool. The different colored LED lights made the water look pretty. Snuggling underneath my wool throw, I took a sip from my wine glass.

Eli took a seat. "Where are my nieces?"

"They finally fell asleep." I chuckled. "What you doing here?" I looked at my brother.

"Shit, just dropping by." He reached for the bottle of Patrón. "That nigga, Tone, been on a war path." He sighed before taking a drink from the bottle. "That nigga's trippin'." Eli looked stressed.

"Oh yeah?" I sipped from my glass.

He relaxed in his seat. "Trippin' hard. Got niggas scared to even come around him. He beat the fuck outta Lucus for laughing when he was talking."

"Daisy's son? His cousin?" I asked for clarification.

Eli nodded.

Mmm...

"Nigga chopped two of the lil' homies' fingers off."

I almost choked on my drink.

"Then fed 'em to Diablo," he stated, referring to Tone's red-nose pit. Eli took another drink. "Got the lil' homies spooked."

I stared at the water.

I knew exactly why Santonio was on a rampage. He was hurting. Instead of dealing with his pain like a *sane* person, he was lashing out at everyone around him. He was harming innocent people, making others miserable. I sighed.

"Talk to him, E."

I frowned. "No."

Eli drank from the bottle.

"I hate that y'all going through it, but I'm not putting my happiness on the line to accommodate y'all." Eli had me all types of fucked up.

He smacked his lips. "The shit is causing a strain with me and Sash."

I shrugged.

"Yvonne too. Peyton talking 'bout she pregnant again."

I stared at him. "*What*?"

He couldn't even look at me.

"You didn't." I grilled him. "I *know* you didn't." Peyton was Eli's second baby mama. The same bitch he swore up and down he couldn't stand.

"Shit just happened." He took a long drink from the bottle.

"You are so fuckin' selfish." I gripped my glass tightly. "Why the fuck are you still fuckin' all *three* of your baby mamas?!" I yelled. "What about Sasha, my friend?!"

Eli ran his hand down his face in an aggravated manner.

"You are so disrespectful." I chuckled condescendingly. "You don't respect mama, your babies' mamas, or your sisters." I sat my glass on the table. "You don't care about nobody but yourself." Once Sasha found this out, our friendship was over. Yeah things between us were fucked up, but we were just going through a rough patch. I felt deep down Sasha and I could get past all of this. We'd been through worse.

"That ain't true."

"You sure?" I asked, tilting my head. "You knocked up my best friend. One of the only people I could count on." I stared at him. "You put me in a fucked up position."

"The shit just happened." He shrugged.

"Do you love her?"

"I don't know." He took another gulp.

I knew what that meant. No.

"Why are you stringing her along?" We both knew who really held the key to his heart; Peyton, his first love.

Peyton had been smart enough to not fall for Eli's bullshit. Once they ended their relationship, she moved to Chicago. He'd had a long distance relationship with my nephew for years until she moved back six months ago.

"I care about Sash."

"But you don't love her." She'd given him a set of twin boys who were a little older than Sanaa, and he still didn't appreciate her.

"What's with the third degree?" He frowned. "You acting like I don't give a fuck about her."

"'Cause you *don't*, Eli." I leaned forward. "How do you think Sasha is going to take this news?"

I felt bad for my friend. She was in love all by herself. I was sure Eli, being the womanizer that he was, had her clueless. Like I said, outside of the women in his family, the only chick he ever cared about was Peyton. Don't get me wrong, Peyton was a cool chick, but when she dipped to Chicago with Elijah, Eli hurt behind that for a long time. I should've known once she decided to come back after her sister's funeral, Eli would be right back in her bed.

"We gon' work it out. She'll be a'ight," the dummy had the gall to say with a straight face.

"*She'll be alright*?" Even though now wasn't the time to laugh, I thought about that mocking SpongeBob meme. I had to repeat it back to him so he could hear how stupid he sounded.

"I didn't come here to be chastised, Erin." He leaned back further into his seat. "Between my babies' mamas, a nigga argues enough. I'm tryna chill for a second." That was his way of telling me to drop it because he was done with the discussion.

Shaking my head, I reached for my glass again and stared back at the water. "You need to tell her *soon*."

"I will."

Taking a long sip from my Patrón and cranberry juice, I relaxed in my seat.

"That nigga hit you?"

My eyes rolled to Eli who was staring at me intensely.

"No."

"What happened to your lip?"

"Hit my face on the car door."

Eli stared at me for a long while before he said, "That nigga, Tone, is testing my patience, bro." He sipped from the bottle again.

"Eli, he didn't hit me."

"He pushed you?"

I sighed and he smacked his lips.

"That nigga touch you again, he gon' have to see me." He shook his head. "Nah, I'ma have to rap wit' that nigga tonight."

"Eli..." I groaned. "Let it go. He didn't hit me and he apologized for pushing me. We're not even talking right now because he knows he fucked up." I wasn't trying to overlook the fact that Santonio was wrong, I just wanted to keep the peace. My brother beefing with my baby daddy wasn't a good look. They were both nutty as hell and my heart couldn't bear anything happening to either one of them off the strength of me.

Eli looked like he wanted to say something else, but he sighed instead. His long dreads swayed as he shook his head, eyeing me.

"Promise you won't start trippin' with Santonio." I stared at him.

He looked up at the sky.

"Eli, promise me," I pressed. I had enough shit going on in my life. I didn't need them adding to my stress.

"I promise," he replied, still looking up at the stars.

"Thank you. You talk to Erica?" I asked, switching the subject.

"Nah."

"You should call her." Our baby sister was wilding out. She'd been fighting, disrespecting our mama, and spending days away from home whenever they get into it. We were supposed to be meeting up at the gym tomorrow. I only hoped Erica wouldn't make me act ugly.

"I'll holler at her. I know her grown ass is fuckin' now." Eli grimaced and I chuckled.

"I mean she *is* at that age." I still remember when Eli found out I was having sex. He locked himself in his room for two days and didn't come out unless he had to use the restroom.

"Fuck outta here." He waved me off uninterested. "Erica needs to stay in them books. She's too smart to go out like a dummy."

"We'll be together tomorrow. After we leave the gym, we're going out to lunch. You should meet us there." I shrugged.

He nodded. "A'ight."

We sat silent for a moment, both lost in our thoughts. I'm sure Eli was contemplating on whether or not he was going to go back on his promise. I knew my brother, though. He never made a promise he couldn't keep. Growing up after watching Scarface for the first time, he'd always tell me all he truly had in this world was his balls and his word. Eli was a lot of things, but he never went back on a promise.

Fall leaves swept across the grass, making me relax deeper into my seat. Just like the season was changing, so were my relationships with some of the people I held dearest to my heart. I only prayed I would continue to stay strong through whatever.

TONE

"Don Capporelli..." I hit the cigar secured between my index finger and thumb. Leaning back in my office chair, I took a puff.

"Santonio, how are you?" Don Capporelli's voice was low on behalf of the nigga not being able to open his mouth all the way. He'd gotten shot in the cheek back in the day and his speech had been fucked up ever since.

"Everything's straight on my end." I relaxed further in my seat. The dim lights in my office put me in a mellow mood. I didn't feel like talking to the nigga. He hadn't called for friendly conversation. I already knew what he wanted.

"I spoke with my son."

I chuckled.

"He says there's been an altercation."

"With who?"

Don Capporelli chuckled.

It was like I was doing business with a bunch of bitch-ass, snitching-ass niggas. Any beef Bruce or Hakim had with me should be settled with *me*. I wasn't hiding and they knew where to find a nigga. After I sent Deidra to get the tapes from *Coacoa*, Que went looking for

Hakim and ended up finding out he had hopped on a flight back to Portland. I already knew Bruce wouldn't let what happened slide.

I was cool with that, though.

"The issues between Bruce and you are becoming, eh... What's the word? A nuisance?" His broken English was starting to annoy me.

I took a puff. I was a grown-ass man. I didn't care shit about what Don Capporelli was yapping about. My office door opened and Roman stepped in followed by Que. Que took a seat in a free chair and Ro swaggered over to the bar. Tugging at my beard, I waited for Don Capporelli to get to his point.

"Questo non sarà un problema continuo, vero?

"I ain't the one wit' the problem."

"This will be the last time I hear nonsense." His muffled tone rose a little.

"From *me*?" I couldn't speak for the next man.

Don Capporelli chuckled. "I will talk to you later, Santonio." And with that, he hung up.

I tossed my phone onto my desk and looked at Que and then Ro. "What y'all niggas want?"

Roman took a seat at the bar holding a glass filled with brown liquor. "Don't start that cry-baby shit today."

Que chuckled.

"Fuck all that." I didn't care that everybody was walking on eggshells around me. I didn't care that I'd beaten the fuck out Lucus and now Ma Duke was mad at me. I didn't give a fuck that the lil' homies were scared to come around me. "What the fuck y'all want?" I frowned.

Roman was my first cousin, but more like a kid brother. He was probably the only nigga who felt comfortable talking shit to me. Nah, he was the *only* nigga. I was only two years older than him, but growing up I'd taken on the role of big bro. Everybody thought we had a lot of similar features, but I was sure it had a lot to do with our mothers being sisters. Roman drank coolly from his glass and ignored me.

My eyes shot to Que.

"Them lil' niggas from the east trippin'." He shrugged. "Went down north and lit some shit up." He took a pre-rolled blunt from behind his ear and then reached in his pocket for a lighter.

"The fuck you tellin' me for?" I hit my cigar again.

"You know the east side feel like they ain't gotta follow the same code as everybody else," Roman spoke up. "Them niggas know what's up."

I shook my head. I was from the east and everybody knew it. The lil' homies down there worshipped me, but they were always pressing hard lines with other hoods. They knew I fucked with the east side the long way, so they felt like they should get special privileges. It was my own fault because I still kicked it in the hood sometimes but only on my side, though.

"If them lil' niggas wanna kill each other, let 'em." I shrugged.

Que sighed.

"That's bad for business." Roman finished off his drink. "Who gon' run dope and shit if you got the workers killin' each other off?"

"You niggas..." My eyes darted back and forth between each mug. "Y'all can't control y'all teams, then maybe I need some new captains."

Roman glared at me. Que ran his hand across the top of his head in annoyance. But neither one of them niggas said a word. I smirked. I put my cigar out and then reached for my ringing phone.

"Yeah?"

"Hey, Tone?"

"Who's this?"

She chuckled. "I thought you were a sweet heart?"

I hung up the phone. I knew who it was. I hadn't spoken to Brandi since I fucked her the night I met her. She was a cool chick, but I didn't feel like dealing with her. There were two taps on my office door and then it opened. The home girl, Faith, stepped in.

"Hey, Tone, Eli is downstairs." She smiled.

I pushed back from my chair, stood up and grabbed my heat off my desk. I tucked it into my jeans and stalked out of my office with Roman and Que behind me. I walked through my chop slash auto shop, acknowledging a few workers before I made it to the front where Eli was standing with Silas. I approached him and we slapped fives cordially, but I could see the anger behind his eyes. I widened my stance.

"Wassup?"

He stared at me. "You hit my sister." He flexed.

Roman stepped up further.

I crossed my left arm against my chest and stroked my beard with my right. "Is that what she told you?" She didn't. If I knew E, she'd said the exact opposite.

"That's your baby mama, but she's my sister." He grilled me.

"What you tryna do?" I didn't wanna kill Eli because he was my boy. But I would and then sleep like a baby.

"E done been through enough. I'm tired of seeing my sister hurt."

I nodded.

"You my nigga, but I'll die for my sister."

I could respect that. 'Cause I'd die for her stubborn ass too.

"Let me handle my shit with Erin, a'ight?"

He looked back and forth between Que and Roman. I could tell that there was more he wanted to say. Erin had probably made him promise to stay cool. "Yeah, a'ight."

I chuckled before stepping around him. "Everybody meet me on the east side in thirty minutes," I said over my shoulder as I made my way towards the glass exit. "Somebody call True."

13

I LIED

ERIN

"Come to Swope with me please," Chance asked as soon as I opened my front door for her.

I frowned. "Uh, no." I started through my foyer and she closed the door.

"Erin, seriously?" She followed me. "This is the last time until next summer that it's gon' be this lit."

"I'm good." I knew Santonio would be there. I hadn't seen or spoken to him since we'd sat in the shower, holding each other for the last time. That was almost three weeks ago. Whenever he wanted Sanaa or Toni, he'd pick them up from Sadee's and drop them off at my mom's afterwards. We'd pass messages through our mothers and keep it pushing.

"Come on," Chance pressed. "I know your ladybugs are with Ms. Sadee, so you're kid free for the weekend."

"That's why I plan on using that time to relax." We made it to my kitchen.

"So, you're really going to make me go by myself?" she asked in disbelief.

I rolled my eyes. Chance was a spoiled brat. Thanks to True, "*no*" was a foreign word to her.

"Where's Morgan and Ava?" I took a seat at the island.

"Morg is in Connecticut and Ava isn't answering the phone," she pouted. "E, you *have* to go with me. Who gon' have my back if I'm out there with them jealous hoes all by myself."

I gave her the side eye. Chance knew damn well if True was anywhere near, wasn't shit happening to her.

"Okay, look." She paused, trying to come up with a different approach. "Hang wit' me for one hour."

I sighed.

"One hour, E. I really wanna go, but I don't wanna go by myself. True took the doors off my Jeep and had some new speakers put in." She smiled. "I got a cooler in the back filled with Mang-o-ritas." She danced.

I chuckled. It didn't take much for Chance to get drunk.

"You don't even have to get all cute," she continued trying to sell me. "What you have on is perfect."

I looked down at my black ripped skinny jeans and the velvet Fenty slash Puma sneakers on my feet. My black boyfriend tee had a dope picture of Kendrick Lamar on it, and my hair was pulled up into a tight bun. The only jewelry I had on were the gold hoops in my ears and my diamond studded nose ring.

Chance was sporting a white Royals jersey, jeans, and blue Chuck Taylors to match. Her hair sat high in a loose ponytail. The big, gold bamboo earrings in her ears meshed well with the thin gold necklaces around her neck. Chance reminded me of Lauren London, only she was shapely. She had the deep dimples and everything.

I rolled my eyes. "Try calling Ava again." I wasn't going to Swope.

Chance sat her purse down on the island. "If I call her and she doesn't answer, will you go?"

"No." I frowned.

Rolling her eyes, she put her phone on speaker and we listened to it ring. When Ava's voicemail picked up, Chance ended the call and stared at me with sad eyes. "One hour, E."

I groaned.

~

I SAT in the passenger's seat of Chance's Jeep with a Mang-o-rita in one hand and weed vapor in the other. Nikki Minaj's "LLC" joint was bumping loudly as Chance stood in front of the Jeep giggling in some dude's face. The weather was surprisingly nice for the second week of November. Swope was packed with men who were trying to show off their souped-up rides and women who were trying to bag a baller. Somebody even started up one of the parks grills and started grilling.

> ♫*Niggas gassed on it, really though, gas I pump them*
> *Straight trash on the really, yo, yes, I dumped him*
> *Push the limits, I'm a pushy bitch, yes, I bumped him*
> *Push past being filthy rich, ask I trumped them*♫

I bobbed my head, finishing off the rest of my wine cooler. Hopping out of the Jeep, I headed for the trunk to get another one. The loud sounds of motorcycles and hemi's approaching made me look in the direction of all the noise. At least ten different muscle cars, ranging from Camaros to Chargers and Challengers, were speeding through the park with bikes zooming behind them.

I rolled my eyes.

Bitches started slowly making their way towards the other side of the parking lot. I grabbed the bottle of D'usse I had Chance stop and get, popped the seal and took a long drink.

"You okay?" Chance came to the passenger's side and asked as I retook my seat in the Jeep.

I nodded.

"True and them are here."

"I know."

She sighed. "You ready?"

Shaking my head, I chilled back against the plush seat. "Nah, I'm good."

"Okay." Her eyes roamed in their direction. "Oh, here comes Ava." She smiled.

I took another sip.

"I was hoping you bitches would be here," I heard Ava before I saw her.

I chuckled.

Chance cheesed. "I've been calling you all day, heffa."

Ava approached the passenger's side. "Roman was trying to keep me hostage in our bedroom." She blushed and then nudged me. "What? You can't speak?"

I passed her the bottle. "What's up, Av?"

She pouted playfully. "You just said fuck me, huh?" She took a drink from the bottle and danced playfully.

I hit my vapor a few times and then handed it to her.

Chance took the bottle of D'usse and took a long gulp.

"The niggas is out, yo." Ava grinned.

I laughed. "Roman will set this park on fire."

She shrugged. "I'm allowed to look."

Chance gave her a yeah-right look. "Ava, please be on your best behavior," Chance scolded.

Ava was the home girl with no filter, just looking to have a good time. She was the one you had to have the "pep talk" with before you left the house. You had to remind Ava's crazy ass: no fighting and no tasing. Every time we all hung out, you could count on Ava to make it a night to remember. Her antics were violent, but funny as hell.

Ava handed me the vapor back. "Chance, don't start with me. You need to be giving True that same speech."

We vibed to the music and caught up. Eventually, I hopped out of the Jeep and we started cracking jokes back and forth. Chance got drunk and wanted to dance, making us all laugh when her thick ass started dropping it like it was hot. We almost got into a fight when Ava asked some chick what she was looking at. After smoking the weed up and finishing off a few more wine coolers, we were feeling ourselves.

"Y'all come wit' me right quick." Ava started towards the thick crowd of people in the parking lot.

Chance grabbed up her wine cooler, and I put my arms through my jean jacket.

It's about to be some shit. Just watch.

TONE

Leaning against my whip, I took a drink from the double Styrofoam cup in my hand. Me and my niggas had Swope jumping as usual. Music was playing from every car and motorcycle. Weed and liquor were being passed around just like the bitches were. I preferred the lean in my cup and the blunt in my hand that I wasn't sharing.

"True, I swear to God!"

My eyes rolled over to Nisha, True's bitch. She was always trippin' and shit.

"Nish, man, move." He pushed her away from him.

"Answer me!" she screamed.

I took a sip from my cup and scanned the crowd. When my eyes landed on Erin's pretty face, my heart did a back flip in my chest. The mean look on her face might've intimidated other niggas, but it turned me on. E didn't take no shit, and she made sure you knew off the flip she wasn't to be fucked with. She licked her lips as her eyes skidded across the sea of people. Then her gaze landed on me.

We locked eyes for a minute. I hit her with a quick head nod, and she gave me a side smile. She then faced Chance and Ava. I lit my blunt, put it to my lips and took a toke.

"Hey, stranger."

I looked to the left of me to see Brandi. "Wassup?" I eyed her.

"You hung up on me the other day."

"I was busy."

Brandi laughed. "You could've at least said bye." She flipped her dreads back.

I shrugged.

"Fuck you, Chance!" My eyes rolled back in Nisha's direction. She now had her finger in Chance's face.

Erin pushed her and I rose off my ride. Hitting my blunt, I made my way over to her. Brandi followed me.

"Erin, this ain't got shit to do with you!" a chick standing next to Nisha hollered.

"Bitch, shut up!"

"Ava..." Roman pulled her towards him.

"We all know you probably fuckin' her fat ass!" Nisha yelled in True's face. In return he snatched her up by her shirt and dragged her way.

Nisha's home girl charged at Chance and stole on her. Erin slugged home girl from the side, causing her to stumble back and then they started banging. I dropped the blunt and cup. Erin started dragging ole girl across the lot, punching and stomping her. I grabbed her. She wouldn't let up, though.

E somehow got a hold of her hair and wouldn't let go.

I held her. "Erin, let go."

She tugged harder and then kicked the girl.

"Aaagh! Let me go!" home girl cried.

I tried to yank Erin away and ole girl came too; crying loudly because E had a death grip on her hair. The bottom of E's Puma came down hard on her face.

"Erin!" I started prying her fingers from the chick's head. Finally, I was able to pull her away, but not without a fistful of shorty's hair.

I hadn't even noticed nosey muthafuckas in the parking lot had turned their music down. Volumes went back up as the crowd spread for me to get by. With Erin still in my arms, I made my way back to my ride. Pinning her rowdy ass up against the driver's door, I gripped her face firmly. Wrapping my free hand around her waist, I held her still.

I then looked down into her face. "Calm down."

She tried to turn away from me, only making me squeeze her cheeks tighter.

"Let me go," she growled through pursed lips.

I stared hard into her face and her body relaxed. Placing my lips on her forehead, I took a deep breath. "I don't want you out here fighting. I'm in a good head space right now so don't make me kill one of these bitches for puttin' their hands on you," I said calmly.

She nodded knowingly.

I let her go, took a step back, and looked her over slowly. The bun in her hair sat lopsided, so I pulled the loose ponytail holder out of her hair. Eyeing her, I ran my hands through her hair and licked my lips. She looked down and started running her fingers through her mane. When she looked back up at me, we stared at one another.

Erin looked to the right of her and frowned.

I followed her gaze to Brandi. I hadn't even realized she was standing there. I turned my fitted cap backwards. "Wassup?"

"We were talkin'." Brandi glanced at Erin.

Erin sucked her teeth and tried to get around me. I wrapped my arms around her lower body.

"What you mad for?" I looked down at her.

"Really?" she asked in disbelief. "One of your many bitches is standing here."

"That ain't my bitch. I don't even know her." Shit, I didn't know nothing but her name.

Brandi stomped away.

Erin crossed her arms. "I know you fucked her."

I tugged at my beard. "I ain't trippin' off her." The parking lot started jumping again.

She rolled her eyes.

"What you doin' out here anyway?" I stepped away from her. "I thought you spent weekends cooped up in the house reading them ghetto ass books."

She laughed. "I don't read ghetto books. I don't even know what that is." She snickered.

"Yeah, a'ight." I eyed her. "Moms told me Toni crawled all the way to the door."

Nodding, she pouted. "I told her to slow down. Sanaa's already two going on twenty-two."

I chuckled. "Sanaa acts just like her mama. She's moody. Toni's sometiming ass is mean too."

Erin hit my arm. "Don't do my babies." She bucked at me playfully and I faked a flinch, making her laugh.

"Toni-noni tryna make room for another one."

Erin stared at me. "Don't play with me."

I laughed. Licking my lips, I ran my hand down my mouth. "You don't wanna have my baby?"

She smacked her lips. "I got *two*. It'll be just my luck I get another girl." She kicked a rock.

"Get yo lazy ass on top then."

Erin cracked up. "I get on top. Don't come for me."

I took my hat off and ran my free hand across my waves before I put it back on. "Yeah, a'ight." I was only fuckin' with her. E loved riding dick.

She shook her head.

"You need anything?" I'd already had Ma Duke and her moms ask for me a couple times, but I wanted to hear it with my own ears.

"Nope."

I stared at her. "You know I'm the first person you can call on, right?" I eyed her. "You can call me for anything whether we're together or not."

She nodded. "Yeah, I know."

I ran my thumb across her jaw and she exhaled slowly.

"I'll pick up the ladybugs from my mom's at three on Sunday." She stepped around me.

I watched her walk towards Chance and Ava. She said something to the duo and then Chance followed her across the parking lot. They got in Chance's whip and drove out of the park.

14

HELL IS OTHER PEOPLE

ERIN

"Sanaa, I'ma tell yo mama." I heard Erica say as I rounded the corner.

"So!" Sanaa's little squeaky voice shot back.

I entered her room. "What y'all in here arguing about?"

Erica and Sanaa acted like sisters instead of auntie and niece.

"Your daughter is a bully." Erica threw a bear at Sanaa. "She tryna kick me out her room."

"I mean you are lying across her bed like it's yours." I bounced Toni in my arms.

"I get the best signal in her room for some reason," she said with her phone to her ear.

"Sanaa, you wanna help mommy bake cookies?" I asked.

"No," she pouted.

"You sure?" I dropped down into a squatting position and she dragged her feet as she made her way to me.

Her glossy eyes made me look at Erica.

"Get out of my baby's bed."

"What?!" Erica frowned. "I'm not bothering her."

"Yes, you are."

Erica sucked her teeth, but hopped off the bed. "I'm 'bout to go home then."

I shrugged and stood up. "When you get there tell Mama I said call me. She's supposed to watch Sanaa and Toni tomorrow so I can go run a couple errands."

They followed me down the hallway.

"I'm not tellin' her nothin'. I can't even lie in a bed. Why are your kids so spoiled?"

I chuckled. "My kids aren't spoiled. They're *loved*." I grabbed a hold of Sanaa's hand as I helped her down the stairs.

"Same thing. I'm spending the night."

"I thought you were leaving?"

Erica laughed. "Psych. Hello?" she finally spoke to whoever she was on the phone with.

We hit the landing and I started for the family room.

"Mommy, are you makin' cookies?" Sanaa asked, still holding my hand.

I nodded. "Yep."

She let me go and rushed to her American Girl doll that was sitting on the couch.

Just as I put Toni in her walker, I could hear tires coming to a loud screech in my driveway.

What the fuck?

Erica ran to the window and pulled the curtain to the side.

"Who is that?"

"Sasha and Eli. But they're in two different cars," she stated, confused. "They're arguing and he's trying to get her back in the car."

I pulled my hair up and wrapped it in a bun. "Take Sanaa and Toni back upstairs for me." I started out of the room.

"Sasha fonkin' with you?"

I ignored her. Once I made it to the front door, I pulled it open and I immediately heard Sasha and Eli arguing.

"Get back in the car, dawg."

'Let go of me!" she screamed back.

I shut my front door and made my way down the steps. "What's going on?"

Sasha's piercing eyes landed on me. "You knew!"

I looked to Eli. "Knew what?"

"Don't act dumb, Erin! You knew Peyton was pregnant, but you didn't tell me!"

"It wasn't her business to tell!" Erica screamed from behind me. I hadn't even heard the front door open. "I'm tired of you coming for my sister like she won't fuck you up, Sasha!"

"Erica, go back in the house." Eli yanked a fighting Sasha towards his car.

I faced her. "Erica, please go check on my babies."

Blowing out a deep breath, she went back inside and slammed the door.

I approached Sasha and my brother. "Sasha, you came here to do what?"

"E! Go back in the house!"

"No!" I yelled back. "She pulled up and hopped out like there's an issue, so let's fix it."

Sasha got hyped. "What's up, bitch?! These other bitches might be scared of you, but I'm not!"

I damn near started sprinting to get to her. I cocked my fist back, swung and hit Eli instead because he blocked her body.

"Aye!" He shoved me hard and I landed on my ass. An instant pain surged through my backside. "I can't let you hit on my baby mama, E. You know that." He looked conflicted.

"I know you did not just push my sister for that bitch!" Erica screamed, rushing towards us.

I hopped up from the stone driveway and charged at Eli. Everything around me went black as I punched him repeatedly. I'd kept *his* secret, destroying the relationship with *my* best friend. And I had still ended up with the short end of the stick.

I was shocked, angry, confused, and hurt.

"Erin!" I heard Erica, but I couldn't see her. I couldn't see past my brother dogging me and Sasha disrespecting me.

As Erica pulled me away, I yanked at his shirt.

"Pussy, don't you ever put your fuckin' hands on me!" I punched him in the head. I started tagging the shit out of him when I felt Erica let me go.

He tried to block my hits, but I was in a rage.

"Erin!" He finally wrapped me in a bear hug. "Chill."

My chest heaved up and down.

"Bitch, you see what you did!" Erica screamed at Sasha who I noticed was now silent.

"Mommy!" I heard Sanaa crying.

Hearing her cry made me cry. And I guess seeing me cry made Erica cry.

"Let my sister go, Eli." I knew her tears were from frustration just like mine were. I'd never fought my siblings. I could never put my hands on them whether it was a push, pull, slap, or punch.

All our lives it had been the three of us. When our mom checked out on us for a while after our dad left, it was us. When my grandma suggested my mom split us up in the family, and Eli stepped up to the plate, it was just us stuck together like the Three Musketeers.

I snatched my body away from Eli and went to see about Sanaa who was bawling her eyes out. I picked her up and rushed inside. I entered the family room and sighed when I saw Toni was still sitting in her walker. I heard the door shut and then footsteps approaching. Sanaa was still crying as I tried to console her.

"Is she okay?" Erica asked.

I nodded. "Naa..." I kneeled down. "Mommy's okay."

She cried harder. Like I said, Sanaa was my sensitive baby. She'd never gotten a whooping, hardly ever got yelled at, and she'd never seen a fight. I wasn't sure all of what she had seen, but my ladybug was upset. Her tear-stained face broke my heart.

Yeah, Sasha gon' have to feel me.

"I want my daddy!" Sanaa cried louder, which scared Toni and made her cry too.

"Shhh..." I hugged her. "Stop, Naa. Be Mommy's big girl."

"I want my daddy." She hugged my neck tight.

"Erica, get my phone off the table and call Tone."

TONE

"I want a bowl from Chipotle."

"That shit is trash." I scrolled through my phone from the passenger's side of Deidra's Range.

"Nigga, you trippin'. Chipotle is fire."

I shook my head. When my phone started ringing and I saw it was Erin, I immediately became alarmed. Erin hadn't called my phone in over a month.

"E, what's up?"

"Tone." Her little sister Erica responded instead.

"Where's Erin?" I could hear crying in the background. I sat up in my seat. "Put Erin on the phone."

"She's trying to calm Sanaa and Toni down." She sounded aggravated.

"Put her on the phone!"

She fumbled with the phone a little.

"Swing by E's real quick." I told Deidra and she nodded.

"Here." I heard Erin say.

"Daddy?" Sanaa's soft voiced came through, followed by a sniffle.

"What's wrong, Naa-Naa?" I knew I sounded like a punk when I asked, but my baby didn't cry. Sanaa was so innocent that it scared me sometimes because I knew as she got older, muthafuckas would take her sweetness for granted.

She started crying.

"Stop crying." I looked out my window. "Tell Daddy what happened."

"My mommy fell." She sniffled.

"Mommy fell?" I asked, confused.

"Yes."

I sighed. "Stop crying, Naa. Didn't Mommy tell you big girls don't cry?"

She sniffled. I listened on as she tried to get herself together. I knew it was her idea to call me in the first place. Sanaa knew that if she had any problems, Daddy would fix them. She was still a baby, but she'd learned that concept early on.

"I love you, Naa-Naa."

"I love you too."

"Put Mommy on the phone." I waited for Erin.

"Hello?"

"Why is Sanaa crying?"

"Because she saw me fighting."

I frowned. "Who?"

She paused.

"Where were you fighting?"

"At home."

I nodded. That meant it was somebody close to her. Erin didn't let just anybody come to her house.

"Who hit you?"

"He—"

"*He*?!"

"Eli and—"

"That nigga put his hands on you?!"

"No, he pushed me."

"And you fell?" I was fuming.

"Santonio—"

I hung up the phone. I scrolled through my contacts until I found

Eli's name. Deidra tried to hand me the blunt, but I shook my head no. Tugging at my beard, I waited for him to answer. When he did, he was arguing.

"Tone—"

"You pushed my baby?"

"What?"

"You pushed *E*?" I clarified.

"Tone, man..." He sighed. "I was trying to keep her and Sasha apart."

"So, you pushed her and she fell in front of my daughter?"

The line went quiet.

"Where you at?"

"Tone."

"Where you at, Eli? I need to rap wit' you in person."

Deidra hung her head and shook it.

"I'm at my Ma Duke's so I—"

I ended the call. "Take me to Veronica's." I leaned back in my seat.

~

When Deidra pulled up in front of Veronica's spot, she was standing on the porch smoking a cigarette. I hopped out the whip and Deidra followed suit.

"Tone, don't bring that mess over here." She looked stressed. "Let Eli and Erin figure it out. Siblings fight."

"Fuck all that." I removed my strap from off my side and passed it to Deidra.

"That's her brother."

"Tell that nigga to come outside."

"Tone..." Veronica looked like she was on the brink of a break-down. "Don't do this."

I chuckled. "Go get that nigga or I'ma go get him myself."

She put her phone to her ear.

I nodded, making my way towards the house. Just as I was

climbing the steps, Eli came out. When he saw me, he shook his head and ran his hands down his face.

"What's going on?" Sasha came out next. When she saw me, she did a three-sixty and went right back inside.

"Come holla at me, E." I crossed my arms and widened my stance.

He hesitated at first.

"Sadee," Veronica spoke into her phone. "Santonio is in my yard trippin'. Please come get him."

Eli made his way to me. "Tone, I ain't tryna beef wit' you, dawg."

When he got within' arms reach, I rocked his jaw. His head flew back. Before he could recover from the first punch, my fist crashed into his nose. Blood squirted all over his shirt as he stumbled a little before swinging back and missing. I stole on him two more times and he staggered around, swinging mindlessly.

"Tone!" Veronica was crying now.

My right hook jerked his head back and my left swing busted his lip. He sent a blow to my body before wrapping his arms around me. He tried lifting me up and body slamming me, but I elbowed him hard in his back. He let me go, still swinging, but not connecting.

"Stop!" Veronica tried to run up on me and Deidra grabbed her.

My last punch sent his bitch ass tumbling down. He laid in the grass in a daze.

I stalked towards Deidra. "Gimme' dat." My chest rose up and down violently.

Her eyes went sad. "Tone, stall 'em out."

I snatched my gun from her.

"Please!" Veronica started screaming. "Tone, please!" she cried.

Grabbing Eli by his shirt, I dragged him to the street.

"Deidra! Please," Sasha was now hollering and crying too. "Make him stop."

Once we made it to the curb, I cocked my gun. "Open your mouth!"

Eli coughed. "Fuck you!"

I put the gun on the back of his head. "You chose that hoe-ass bitch over your own sister?" I shook my head and he hung his. "Open your mouth or I'ma blow the back of your dome off, nigga." I chuckled. "Nah, as a matter fact, since it's fuck me..." My voice trailed off as I dragged him right in front of the curb. "Bite the curb." I pressed my gun hard against his temple. I hadn't curbed a nigga in a long time.

"Tone!" Deidra rushed to my side. "Think about what you doin', my nigga. Look where we at," she tried to reason with me.

Tires came to a crazy stop behind me.

"Santonio!" Ma Duke screamed. "Oh my God."

"Tone, look at him." Deidra continued. "You fucked him up. Stall 'em out. Think about Erin. She wouldn't want you to kill her brother." I sucked my teeth and let him go.

"Santonio." Ma Duke grabbed me and I snatched away from her. "Go check on Sanaa. Erin said she's upset." I knew what they were doing. They were using the only people who gave me a peace of mind against me. And it worked.

I made my way back to Deidra's Range as Sasha and Veronica ran to Eli's rescue. I shut the door and leaned back in my seat. My knuckles were busted and I had blood on my clothes. Deidra hopped in the driver's seat, started the car, and pulled off. I reached for the blunt and the lighter in the ashtray and sparked it up.

15

YOU WERE MY HOPES AND DREAMS

ERIN

"Tone just pulled up." Erica looked at me.

I sighed, mentally preparing myself for the tornado about to whip through my home. Sanaa was on the couch sleeping. I sat on the carpet with Toni in my arms, and she was knocked out too. After Sanaa talked to her daddy she was content. She laid down on the couch, wrapped herself in the throw, and fell asleep. Toni, however, saw her sister crying and refused to relax. I had to rock her slowly and whisper sweet nothings to make her calm down.

I heard the front door open and close and waited for Santonio to make his entrance. When he did, the menacing scowl on his face made me look away. I'd talked to Ms. Sadee. I knew all about the altercation with Eli at my mom's. The blood on his white tee was a dead giveaway.

He swaggered into the room like he wasn't covered in blood and took a seat on the couch. Erica left the room. I held Toni tighter and glanced up at Sanaa.

"I wanted to come and check on her." He stared at Sanaa too.

"She's fine," I assured him. "You know how Sanaa is." I kissed Toni's chunky cheek. "She's sheltered."

He laid his head back against the couch.

"You didn't have to do my brother like that." I stared at him.

He ignored me.

"In front of my mama, though?"

He continued to ignore me.

"And while all those people stood outside?"

He still ignored me.

I looked down at Toni. "Santonio, you have anger issues." I'd told him more than once he needed to see somebody like a therapist or a shrink who could make him think rationally.

"That nigga pushed you."

"So did you." I flipped my hair over my shoulder. "You pushed me so hard that you busted my lip."

He sucked his teeth. Santonio never wanted to hear his wrongs.

"Eli pushed me on my butt, and you tried to kill him."

"Sanaa saw him do that shit." He kept his head back.

"Santonio..." I sighed. "You're never wrong."

He looked at me. "According to you, I'm always in the wrong."

"Cheating on me *was* wrong. Your lying to me and stringing me along was wrong too." My eyes got misty so I laid my face gently on Toni's head and rocked slowly.

Santonio lived in his own little world.

"You act like a nigga is perfect."

"Can you at least be faithful?!" My voice rose and I closed my eyes.

Only Santonio...

Anybody else I would've ignored or started swinging on.

"You trippin' off old shit."

My head lifted. "Santonio, get out." I got up slowly. With Toni in my arms, I started towards the hallway and up the stairs.

"You kickin' me out 'cause Eli couldn't keep his hands to himself?"

I kept on my journey. He knew damn well that wasn't why I was putting him out.

"That nigga had Sanaa, Toni, *and* you crying," he pressed,

following me with Sanaa in his arms. "I'm supposed to just sit back and let that shit ride?"

"You should've let me handle my brother."

"Nah..."

We walked in silence as we made our way to Toni's room. He stood in the doorway as I laid Toni down in her baby bed. After tucking her in, I turned on her night lamp. Santonio led the way to Sanaa's room, and I leaned against the doorjamb as he got her situated. He said a silent prayer over her and swaggered past me and out of her room.

I stood in Sanaa's doorway for a minute. My life was spiraling out of control. If I didn't get a handle on some shit, I was going to lose myself. Closing my eyes, I thanked God for everything He'd done for me; good and bad because He seemed to be the only one in my corner. After making sure Sanaa's night light was on, I headed to my own bedroom.

When I entered, Santonio was in the sitting area. He was fully clothed, ESPN blasting, head back, and eyes closed. I made my way over to him and stared at him with my arms crossed.

"Santonio..." I licked my lips.

Was it wrong he was turning me on? Was it wrong his thugged-out mentality made my pussy wet? Was it wrong I wanted to kiss all over him and explore his body? Was it wrong I wanted to ride him until the sun came up and...? Nah, I wasn't even about to go there.

Instead, I tapped his knee. "Santonio."

He licked his lips, opening his eyes sluggishly. "Yeah?"

"I'm getting ready to lie down." My whole day had been shot thanks to Eli and his baby mama.

"Go lay down then," he mumbled.

"Are you leaving?" Instead of a demand, my sentence came out like a question.

"Nah." He closed his eyes.

Rolling my eyes, I spun around and went to take a shower.

∽

WHEN I ENTERED MY ROOM, Santonio was still on the sectional asleep. Sitting on the edge of my bed, I dried myself off. My body was sore from falling and fighting. Even after my bubble bath, I still felt beat down. I prayed Toni would sleep through the night.

It seemed like whenever Tone was near, she and Sanaa woke up out of their sleep to get in my bed. I looked over at Santonio who was now stretched out across the sectional. He'd turned the television down and instead of ESPN, the Investigation Discovery channel played lowly. Shaking my head, I rose off my bed and trekked towards the sitting area. With my robe wrapped around me, I stared at him.

The blood on his white T-shirt was disturbing. I knew it was Eli's and I was sure my brother was somewhere hating me. I slumped forward and I placed my face in my hands. It seemed like every time I took one step forward, life pushed me back three. I couldn't win for shit.

Santonio stirred in his sleep, tucking his hand in his pants. When he placed his right hand over his chest, I noticed his bloody knuckles. I stood up and went back into the bathroom. After lathering a wash-cloth with soap and running it under warm water, I rung it out and headed back to Santonio. He was sitting up now, scrolling through his phone.

I sat down on the coffee table. "Let me see your hands."

Tossing his phone, he scooted his body in front of mine and held his hands out.

Gently taking his hands into mine, I examined them. Not only were they bloody, they were bruised.

Eli...

Tears pooled in my eyes.

"I lost control." I looked up to find Santonio staring at me.

Cleaning his hands off, I swallowed back my tears. "You need to talk to somebody."

He sucked his teeth.

"How you react when you're upset isn't normal." I stared at him. "It's not okay for you to physically harm people just because you're mad." I sighed. "Eli has always been loyal to you and Lucus too."

Santonio stared at me.

"Not only are they loyal, but they're *family*."

He nodded.

"Sanaa is sheltered, Santonio."

He sighed.

"You can't try to kill someone every time she sheds a tear." I cleared my throat. "Me either." I knew the real reason he'd overreacted. Even though I wasn't crying when I talked to him, Santonio knew me better than I knew myself sometimes.

When I finished cleaning his hands off, he pulled his shirt over his head and handed it to me. After discarding it and the dirty towel, I washed my hands and stood in the bathroom mirror.

I was tired. I was emotionally drained and mentally exhausted. A part of me wanted to take my babies and disappear for a couple days. I believed in "the storm before the calm." I just hoped I wouldn't drown in my disappointments. I was going through yet another personal growth spurt, only this time, I didn't have anybody to lean on.

TONE

Most people were surprised when I told them I was a reader. I didn't know if it was because of my appearance or what, but a nigga enjoyed a good book. That was probably why I had never been a dumb criminal. My only issue was remembering who wrote the shit I read. But I did read somewhere that "the calm didn't come because the storm was over. It came because you'd moved into the truth."

I lay across the sectional staring up at the ceiling. Did I regret beating Lucus' ass? No. Did I regret wanting to curb Eli? No. Did I go to extremes? Yeah, majority of the time I did. Was a nigga a little dysfunctional? Of course.

I could hear Erin shuffling around by her bed. Still gazing at the ceiling, I placed my arm behind my head. Everything I needed and wanted was with E. My happiness was with her. My past, present, and future belonged to her. She was the only woman who could make a savage cry.

When she tossed a cover on top of me, I looked at her.

"It gets cold over here during the night for some reason." Folding her arms, she walked away.

"Come here, E." I looked back up at the high ceiling.

"What?"

"Come here, man." I sat up.

She rolled her eyes, but backtracked.

"You know I love you, right?"

She remained silent.

"I didn't mean to put you in a fucked up position. I wasn't trying to turn you and your bro against each other."

Her sad eyes danced around me. "It's cool."

I chuckled at her tough ass. I knew better, though. Wasn't shit cool about how I had handled Eli, at least not to her. But Erin would rather weep internally than to let you see any hurt on her pretty face. It was one of the many reasons I fucked with her.

"I won't stop his money." I was only doing that off the strength of me being in love with his sister. Anybody else would've been done.

She nodded.

"I don't want him around my daughters for a while."

She frowned."Santonio, you don't run shit over here."

"My seeds are here, so in a way, I do." I glared at her.

Her eyes burned through me. "That's my brother. Let us figure that out."

I waved her hard-headed ass off. "What's the deal with you and Sasha?"

The stern look in my baby's eyes hurt my feelings. She and Sasha were supposed to be ride or die...tight like sisters. I could remember Erin rushing to Sasha's rescue when her ex had shitted on her. Erin also moved her right on into her home and at one point, gave her *and* the twins rooms of their own. E was always looking out for her people, so I was confused as to why Eli said he had tried to keep her and Sasha apart. Erin didn't just ride for me and her family; she rode till the wheels fell off for everybody she genuinely loved.

"She's mad at me."

I tapped the seat next to me twice and she flopped down, pouting. "Why?"

"Because Eli, just like every male I know, is incapable of being faithful. And it's not like Sasha didn't know that."

I kicked one leg up on the coffee table. When Erin found out about Eli and Sasha, it broke her heart.

"She pulled up and hopped out like she was looking for a fight. I wasn't even trying to go there with her." She tossed her head back and closed her eyes. "It's like every relationship I hold dear to my heart is crumbling." Her voice cracked.

Laying my head back, I looked up at the ceiling. "Or maybe you're just outgrowing muthafuckas." I shrugged.

With her eyes closed, she sighed.

"When I was a young cat on the come up, I was in this clique of about ten niggas." I placed the cover over her. "A bunch of thug-ass youngins who stayed giving muthafuckas the blues."

She chuckled, shaking her head. "I'm not surprised."

"What that mean?"

"Santonio, stay focused." She opened her eyes and turned to look at me.

"We all had one agenda: make money and a lot of it. Unfortunately, some weren't making as much as others. After a while, I noticed niggas started acting funny. One cat ended up in jail and gave a statement to the police. My name came up." He chuckled. "Envy destroyed my whole crew. Instead of niggas waiting on their turn to shine, their hate for me not only cost me my freedom, but their lives too."

Erin snuggled underneath the blanket.

"Sasha is jealous of you, E."

She frowned.

"You've always been the type to go and get it on your own. All your female friends—Jeanette, Skyy, and Sasha, always came to you for answers and looked to you to be the strong one. And that shit is still weird to me 'cause you're the youngest, but you ahead of your time. You independent, so you don't mind being by yourself. You love having people around, but you can shut the world out if you need to."

Erin pulled her legs up onto the sofa.

"You're a leader. And not just by what you say, it's the shit you do. You cut me off for months to make a point, and you did. You proved to me and everybody else you didn't need me, and you still don't. I know you use me for sex, though."

She giggled.

"Kick me out this bitch before a nigga can get his draws on."

She laughed, shaking her head. "Stupid."

"Nah, but for real, you being Sanaa and Toni's mama eases my mind. Gives me one less thing to have to try to delegate and control, 'cause I know they got you to follow. Sasha loves you."

Erin placed the side of her face on my shoulder.

"It's just shit in her life ain't going right, so she's taking it out on you. She knows how you and Eli rock. She's just using that as a crutch instead of talkin' to you about what's really wrong. That house she lives in is Eli's. The cars are his too. The money is all him. Eli is my boy, but he's a stingy-ass nigga." I chuckled. "But I know it's a reason he's like that. We all got our own demons."

"She blamed me for Nette's death."

I sighed. "Jeanette's death ain't nobody's fault but her own."

Erin rose up and mugged me.

"She killed her baby daddy and willingly jeopardized your freedom."

"So, you know who killed her?"

"I didn't say that."

"Then what are you saying?" She was up on her feet now. "You know who did it?"

"Nah."

Her shoulders dropped. "You're lying." Tears lined the brims of her eyes. "I know when you're lying."

I shook my head.

"Who killed her?"

"Erin—"

"*Don't Erin me!*"

"Hi, Daddy." Sanaa's voice made us both look at the door.

E ran her hands through her hair before trekking towards her. "What's the matter, Sanaa?"

I got up from my seat and followed her. When I reached Sanaa, I picked her up and kissed her forehead.

"Daddy, I want some juice."

"Sanaa..." E huffed.

Sanaa's bright eyes stayed on me.

"You want some *water*?"

She shook her head no and I started out of Erin's room.

"Santonio, it's late," E spoke from behind me.

"Go lay down. I'ma give her some water."

Erin sucked her teeth, but spun back around.

I hit the landing with Sanaa still in my arms. "What kinda juice you want?"

16

IRREPLACEABLE

ERIN

Thanksgiving Day...

"SANAA, BE CAREFUL!" I called after her as she rushed up Sadee's driveway.

"Okay!" she yelled back, still running.

With Toni in my arms, I made my way into the house. As soon as I stepped into the foyer, my stomach rumbled from the smell of food. Aretha Franklin played lowly throughout the home as I made my way to the living room. I was greeted by Santonio's aunties Paige and Daisy. Daisy smiled as she met me halfway to get Toni.

I handed her over and then took off my royal blue parka.

"I guess people just don't knock anymore," Paige stated snidely.

Daisy proceeded to remove Toni's coat. "Paige, don't start that mess. Sadee already told you and Macie she wasn't having it today."

I rolled my eyes. I didn't care that Paige didn't like me. Hell, I didn't like her ass either. After Skyy tried to let Derick have a relationship with Skylar and she started tripping, I washed my hands with her.

"Daisy, you got her?" Out of all Santonio's aunties, I liked her the most. She'd never taken a shot at me and I'd never heard anything bad about her other than her drinking habit.

"I'm coming to the kitchen, but yeah, I got my baby." She bounced Toni as we made our way to the hall closet. "Looking just like your daddy. You and Sanaa gon' drive my nephew crazy." She laughed as we started down the hall to the kitchen.

"Is he here?"

"Girl, yes. He and the boys are in the den watching football."

I nodded.

"'Bout time you got here, yo." Ava sat at the kitchen island with a PINK water bottle in her hand.

Sadee chuckled, wiping her hands on a towel. "Well, *excuse* me." She switched to Daisy and held her hands out for Toni who nearly leaped out of Daisy's arms. "I thought I made good company."

Ava snickered. "You know I love you."

"Mmm hum." Sadee nuzzled Toni.

I laughed, going to the cabinet for a glass. "How long have you been here?"

"Not that long." She took a long drink from the bottle.

I grabbed a glass. "What you drinking on?" I asked Ava, standing next to her.

She laughed. "Who said I was drinking?"

I gave her a look and she rolled her eyes at me. "Come out to the car with me. I got something to tell you."

I grabbed my glass. "Sadee, you got—"

"She's fine." Sadee gave me a stern look like I knew better than to ask her if she could keep an eye on Toni. I was sure Sanaa had found her Daddy a long time ago.

Ava led the way back to the front door and we stopped at the coat closet. "I'ma end up cussing Macie's broke, bald-headed, deadbeat-ass out."

I shook my head. It was no secret Roman's mother and Ava couldn't stand to be in the same room for more than five minutes.

"Go say that to her face." Paige walked out of the living room.

"I have," Ava spat back. "So, take yo nosey, shit-starting ass on somewhere!"

"Ava Lane." Roman came out of nowhere followed by Santonio who had Sanaa in his arms.

She rolled her eyes as she put her hands through her coat. "She started with me."

Paige threw her hands up walking away. "I swear y'all bring the ghettoest females y'all can find home. Deidra too."

I slipped my coat on.

"Your auntie got one more time," Ava warned Roman. "*One* and I'ma tase her."

Roman only shook his head.

"Where you goin'?" Santonio finally spoke.

Looking up at him, I licked my lips. Why did my baby daddy have to be so damn fine? It wasn't fair.

"Outside with Ava real fast."

"For what?"

"Santonio, really? I don't have to have a reason to go outside." I tucked Sanaa's jeans back neatly inside of her purple Ugg boots.

"Don't leave," he told me sternly before turning around and going back towards the kitchen.

"You either." Roman looked down at Ava. "And make that your last drink."

"Tuh!" Ava spun around and opened the front door. "You only got one kid, and he ain't even here." Before she could step all the way outside, Roman grabbed her arm.

"You heard what the fuck I said. Don't start that drunk shit."

She rolled her eyes. "Can you let my arm go please?"

Roman pulled her into a hug. "Keep on." He kissed her forehead, let her go and walked off.

We ended up outside sitting in Ava's Wraith. She lit a blunt and we vibed to Teyana Taylor's newest album. After reaching into the backseat, she handed me the Hennessy. After filling my cup up, I relaxed into the plush seats.

"Roman's mama is getting on my nerves, yo." Ava sighed.

I looked over at her. "I don't really know her like that, but since the first time I met her, I got bad vibes from her."

"'Cause the bitch ain't shit." She passed the blunt to me. "I told Roman I would keep it cute, but she be trying me."

I nodded. Thank God Sadee loved me. We'd been tight since day one. She was a superb grandma and a dedicated mother. I didn't have to deal with none of that extra shit.

"Who is that?" Ava asked, staring out of her window.

Sipping from my cup, I followed her gaze to a chick shutting the door to a Range. We sat silent as she flipped her dreads over her shoulder, checked her reflection in the driver's window, and started for the house. I'd never seen her before, but Lucus, and Drake were all in the house, so she could've been here for one of them. Santonio's female cousins, Daisy's daughters, usually spent the holidays with their men's families first and then came. I handed the weed back to Ava and then took another gulp of Henny.

"Is she one of their cousins or sisters?" Ava asked.

I shrugged. "I have no idea. She might be lost."

Ava rolled her window down just as the chick was walking past her car. "Aye!"

I chuckled.

The chick stopped. "Yes?"

I stared at her.

"Who you lookin' for?"

"Ms. Sadee. Does she live here? I go to her church and she invited me over since I just moved here from Detroit." She looked towards the house.

Ava looked at me and I shrugged. Sadee was known for offering invites to people from her church who celebrated the holidays alone.

Without another word, Ava rolled her window up. The chick took off towards the house again. "She better keep her fuckin' crooked-ass eyes to herself."

I laughed. The girl's eyes weren't crooked. She was pretty actually. Her faced was caked in makeup, but she was still a decent-looking chick. Ava was just territorial over Roman.

We continued to chill as we finished off the blunt and I drank the rest of my drink down. By the time we exited the car, I was feeling nice. I wanted to go inside the house and eat. Ava wanted to make a liquor store run, but after reminding her about Roman's small threat, she sucked her teeth and followed me inside.

TONE

"Come eat!" Ma Duke yelled from the den's door.

"Hold on!" My uncle, Laron, yelled back. He was my Aunt Daisy's husband and he was a drunk just like her too.

"*Now* please?" Ma Duke said firmly. "I want us to say grace together."

I got up from my seat and everybody followed me to the kitchen. When I entered, Sanaa was at the table and Toni was in her swing sleep. I looked around the room for Erin just as she entered the room with Ava behind her. Her eyes were low and red, letting me know exactly why they went outside. She switched to Sanaa.

"Let's go wash your hands, Naa-Naa."

"I did." Sanaa looked up at her.

E started out of the kitchen the same time Brandi entered. I frowned. Her eyes landed on me and she smirked. Quickly tugging at my beard, I went after Erin. As I passed Brandi, she touched my arm and I pushed her hand away.

"Do you know him?" That was Ava.

"Ava."

"Nah, I'm just sayin' she touchin' all on him and shit." She and Roman argued as I went looking for E.

I found her in the bathroom washing her hands. I stepped inside, shut the door behind me, and leaned back on it. I tugged at my beard. A nigga really wanted to drag Brandi out by her hair, but this was Ma Duke's crib and I would never disrespect her like that. I knew E wouldn't either, but I still felt like she needed the head's up.

"What's up?" She looked at me through the mirror as she dried her hands off.

"That Brandi chick is here on bullshit."

Her stare hardened.

"I don't even know how she—"

Erin sucked her teeth in annoyance. "She said she was here because Sadee had invited her from church."

I shrugged. Brandi had an agenda and I didn't care enough to know what it was. We fucked *once*.

"So, you fucked her?" Erin turned around to face me.

I licked my lips. "Yeah."

She chuckled, condescendingly. "Move so I can get out."

"Don't let that bitch fuck up our shit."

"Ain't no *our* and ain't no *us*, Santonio! There ain't no *we*!" she screamed. "You can't keep your dick in your pants long enough to even *think* I'd take your stupid ass back!"

I ran my hand across my head.

"Move!" Erin yelled in my face.

"Calm down."

"Calm down?" She sighed. "Santonio, get the fuck out of my way."

"Not until you relax."

"I am relaxed. Now move." She crossed her arms and tapped her left foot in an irritated manner. "Sanaa can stay if she wants, but Toni and I are about to go to my mom's."

"You ain't goin' nowhere."

"Says who?" She mugged me. "You?" Erin scoffed. "Nigga, please. You think I'ma sit at a table and share a meal with a bitch you fuckin'? I knew that bitch looked familiar."

I frowned. "Don't disrespect me." I'd never do no shit like that.

Just because I wasn't going to drag Brandi by her hair didn't mean she wasn't leaving.

"Santonio, move. I asked nicely."

Shaking my head, I stepped to the side to let her by.

Erin stormed out of the bathroom and I followed her back to the kitchen.

"Mom, I'm about to go."

Ma Duke looked at me. "What did you do now?"

I stalked towards Brandi. "Aye, shorty, you gotta go." I grabbed her by her arm.

"What's going on?" Ma Duke asked, confused.

Erin pulled Toni out of her swing. "Sanaa, you staying with Granny?"

I yanked Brandi out of the kitchen.

"Why are you trippin'," she pouted. "I've been calling you."

I ignored her.

"Tone..." she whined. "You're hurting my arm." She tried to pull away.

I yanked her harder.

"My purse! My coat!"

I opened the front door the same time I heard Erin.

"Mom, I'm good. I'll pick them up in a couple hours."

"I swear I didn't know, Erin."

"It's cool."

I tossed Brandi out of the house and slammed the door. I faced Erin as she slipped her parka on. "Where you going, man?" I didn't understand why she was mad at me.

"Santonio, please just let her leave." Ma Duke came to her rescue as usual.

"Nah." I snatched her purse away from her. "She ain't going nowhere. Go sit your spoiled ass down." Let E tell it, she wasn't stunting a nigga. But as soon as a bitch got in my face she started trippin'.

"Don't forget Sanaa can hear you." Ma Duke folded her arms. "Just let her get some air, Tonio." She huffed.

Brandi started banging on the door. "I need my purse and my coat!"

"Lord..." Ma Duke spun around and headed for the living room.

I looked down at Erin. "Take your coat off."

She mugged me. "Keep the purse." She reached into her coat and removed her phone and took off after Ma Duke.

I followed.

Ma Duke walked past me carrying a purse and a coat. "Can't even sit down and enjoy dinner as a family without it being some shit," she mumbled.

My eyes landed on Erin who was sitting on the couch doing something on her phone. Walking over to her, I snatched it out of her hands. "Why the fuck you tryin' me, E."

She hopped up. "Give me my shit!"

I tossed her purse, and yoked her up. "Who the fuck you yellin' at?"

She smacked her lips as I gripped the shoulders of her parka and pulled it down.

"I don't wanna fight wit' you, baby." She looked off. "I didn't know that bitch was coming." Brandi was a scheming-ass bitch who was gon' have to answer to the shit she just pulled.

"I already texted Skyy and told her to come and get me."

I got her coat all the way off and threw it on the couch. "Call her back and tell her you good and you 'bout to eat with your family." I tugged playfully at her ponytail.

"Stop touchin' me."

"Nah, you need to stop letting irrelevant bitches gas yo pretty ass up. You think that bitch could hold a candle to you? Can't no bitch compare to you and how I feel about us. I fucked the bird one time. I don't give a fuck about that hoe." I stared down at her.

It was crazy because we weren't together, but Erin's happiness came before anything else. If she told me to go outside right then and stomp a mud hole in Brandi, I would. I was trying to get us back on track. I wasn't even fuckin' no other bitches. I had tunnel vision and all I could see was my baby.

Erin stared back at me. "Stop embarrassing me."

I nodded. I hadn't done the shit intentionally, but I felt where she was coming from. Me fuckin' off had put her in yet another compromising position.

"Give me my phone." She held her hand out.

I passed it to her and watched as she called Skyy. "Skyy?" She paused. "Girl, yeah. How long you gon' be over there?" Erin looked at me and rolled her eyes. "Let me eat and then we'll be on the way."

I adjusted the necklace around her neck.

She laughed at something Skyy said. "You stupid. Yes, I'm bringing Toni and Sanaa, fool." She walked around me and started back to the dining room. "You just make sure your friend don't try me." She chuckled and I shook my head at her.

17

ALL WE GOT IS US

ERIN

W hen I pulled up in front of my mama's house, I put my car in park and sighed. I hadn't seen her or even talked to any of my family other than Erica since Tone went berserk and tried to kill my brother. I hadn't chosen Santonio over Eli. Hell, I was still mad at Santonio. But what could I do? Keep him away from his kids and not allow them to spend holidays with their family?

Exiting my car, I shut the door and then made my way up the sidewalk. There were a bunch of cars lining the street and I knew my mom's house was packed. My grandmother and grandpa were here until Christmas and they always made sure everybody came together for the holidays. A few of my male cousins were posted up on the porch and they all gave me a quick embrace. I wasn't sure what Eli had told them, but I could feel the tension.

Once I got inside, I heard loud music and laughter. I removed my coat, hung it up, and went looking for my grandpa.

"Well, look who finally decided to show their face!" My mom approached me, giving me the side eye. "Where are my babies?"

"Sanaa fell asleep and Toni was getting sick so I didn't wanna bring her out in the cold."

She frowned. "So, you left them with Tone's side?" The alcohol on her breath was strong.

"Mama, don't start." I sighed. I was tipsy, feeling myself too. I hadn't come to argue with her or anybody else. I wanted to see my grandparents and catch up with my cousins.

"Sadee isn't their only grandma, Erin. You sure know how to call me when you need a babysitter, though." She looked me up and down. "Choosing a nigga over your brother."

"I didn't choose Tone over Eli, Ma." I sighed. I'd just gotten here and I was about to leave already.

"Then what you call it? I haven't seen you or talked to you."

I frowned. Even before the incident, my mom and I never talked every day. It was more like every three or four days. It had been that way for as long as I could remember. We'd never shared that mother-daughter bond. I loved her to death, though.

"You need to go apologize to your brother," she slurred before draping her arm over my shoulders. "He's disappointed in you."

I stepped away from her. "I'm not apologizing to him." If anybody was owed an apology, it was *me*. Sasha was constantly disrespecting me. Eli constantly put me right in the middle of their drama, and I hadn't asked Santonio to lash out.

"You are so selfish, Erin." She sighed. "You..."

"Is that my baby?"

Hearing my grandpa's voice made my heart rate speed up. I hadn't talked to him in a while, but he was one of my favorite people. I faced him and my grandmother who wore a look of disapproval on her wrinkled face.

"Papa." I smiled as he pulled me into a tight hug and gave me a firm squeeze. "I missed you."

"I can't tell," my grandmother started. "You haven't called to check on him since his surgery."

"Now, Velma, cut that shit out, ya hear me?" my grandpa said sternly.

"Hey, Grandma." I stared at her.

"Hello, Erin, dear. Are you still messing with that boy?"

"Where are my grandbabies?" My grandpa cut in. "I want to meet Toni."

I hugged his side. "She has a cold."

He nodded. "We're here for a while, so I'll stop by and see her and Sanaa sometime next week." He kissed my forehead before walking off.

I sighed.

"Your brother is in the kitchen." My grandmother looked me up and down. "Go say sorry so we can move past this."

"I already told my mama I wasn't saying sorry."

"Erin..." My mom shook her head. "Just be the bigger person. Damn, Eli had to go to the hospital. The least you could do is apologize to him."

"I bet if it was that boy she wouldn't hesitate." My grandmother folded her arms.

"You know what?" I spun around. "I don't have to deal with this shit." I'd never put Santonio before anybody in my family, but they were acting like I had. Santonio usually stayed out of my family affairs even though he knew how they could be with me.

"Erin..." My mom followed me. "Stop being so damn difficult."

"Hey, cuz." One of my cousins, Mia, gave me a quick side hug. "When did you get here?" She smiled.

"Not too long ago, but I'm about to go." I snatched my coat back out of the closet.

"Oh." She frowned. "We were going to hit Chance It," she stated, referring to True's bar. "You should ride out with me."

Putting my coat on, I shook my head no. "Maybe next time."

"Okay. Well, don't be a stranger." She gave me hug and then switched away.

"So, you're leaving because I want you to make amends with your brother." My mom wouldn't let up.

"No. I'm leaving 'cause you on bullshit."

"Excuse you , young lady!" my grandma shrieked.

Shaking my head, I stormed out of the house. The cold air stung my face and brought tears to my eyes as I made my way to my car.

"E!" I recognized Skyy's voice and spun around. We met halfway and shared a tight embrace. When we let go, she looked back at the house. "That bad, huh?"

I nodded. "I gotta get the fuck out of here before I end up flipping some shit over."

She chuckled. "Bitch, if you leaving, then I'm leaving too!" She laughed and I knew immediately she was intoxicated.

I shrugged. "Come on."

"Let me go get my coat." She looked past me. "That you?" she asked, referring to my 2019 Chrysler 300.

"Yeah, that's me."

She pushed me playfully. "I see you, E."

"Come on." I headed for my car. "Veronica gon' make me cuss her ass out."

"Okay, let me tell Sasha bye." She took off in the opposite direction.

I rolled my eyes. "Hurry up." I knew how Skyy could get when she got liquor in her. Everybody became her friend and you couldn't get her to stop talking.

"Oh, hush!" she yelled back.

When I finally made it to my car, I heard arguing from the porch. I didn't even stop in my tracks to face the ruckus. Instead, I hopped in my ride, started the ignition, and turned the music up. Everybody was making me out to the bad guy and I was getting sick and tired of it. I was officially done being nice to muthafuckas.

TONE

"This nigga is wild." My cousin Drake laughed. He'd been out of the joint for two weeks now and we'd been bullshitting ever since he touched down.

"I swear to God, the bitch pulled up missing a tooth." Lucus kept on. "And not one of the sides either. Nigga, I'm talkin' about one of the front ones."

All of the men around me erupted into laughter and he even got a slight chuckle out of me. We were posted up at my chop slash auto shop kicking shit. It was only me and my cousins with the exception of Deidra. We hadn't seen her all day. I paused for a moment after that realization.

"Aye, one of you niggas talked to DeDe today?" I looked around the room.

Roman leaned forward in his seat. "Nah, I thought one of y'all had."

I looked to Lucus and he shook his head no. I already knew Drake probably hadn't, even though Deidra was his little sister, so I grabbed my phone off my desk. They sat quietly as I called Deidra and put the phone on speaker. I waited for her to answer, staring down my phone. When her voicemail picked up, my eyes rolled over to Drake.

"Call Auntie." Deidre missed family dinner and Aunt Paige hadn't brought it up. Because of that, I figured Deidra was with her latest bitch for the holiday.

Drake called his mama and Roman put his phone to his ear; probably calling Deidre back. Lucus and I sat silently, staring back and forth between them.

Drake cleared his throat. "Ma, where Deidre at?" I watched his body language. "So, you ain't talked to her?" He looked to me and I stood up.

Roman and Lucas followed suit.

"When was the last time you talked to her?" Drake asked as we made our way out of my office.

I led the way down the steps and a grim feeling washed over me. My breathing slowed. "Lucus, call her again." We hit the landing.

As we got closer to the entrance of the glass building, I noticed Deidra's Range sitting on the far side of the parking lot.

"There she go right there," Roman said pissed off.

I frowned. The cameras in my office were motion censored; they should've come on as soon as she pulled up. We got to the door and stood in it waiting for her to get out.

"The fuck is she doing?" Drake said from behind me.

"Probably on the phone gossiping." Lucus laughed. "Y'all know she still a female at heart."

I went into my back pocket for my phone. Pulling up my security app, I noticed one of the camera screens was black. I looked back at the parking lot. "Call her."

Lucus sucked his teeth, but he started tapping his phone. "Her ass is petty."

"Right." Drake cosigned as I opened the door and stepped outside. "She probably mad 'cause we ate without her. My mama said she's been calling her since last night."

I started towards her Range with Roman right next to me.

"She ain't answering," Lucus called from behind me.

I didn't even care about the cold air as it brushed across my frame.

"The fuck is she doin', man?" Roman mumbled, irritated.

My phone started ringing. Looking down at it, I frowned when I saw it was a call from Bruce. I stopped, looked around, and tapped Roman's shoulder twice. He pulled out his strap and looked back at Drake and Lucus. Answering the phone, I kept my eyes on Deidra's Range.

"Wassup?"

"Happy holidays, Santonio."

"The fuck you want?" I frowned.

"Just sending love from Portland."

Hanging up the phone, I continued to Deidre's Range. Her arm hung out of the window, which meant she was probably airing her car out from cigarette smoke. Her body looked to be leaned back against the seat, which raised an instant alarm. I was maybe twelve strides away when her car blew up and burst into flames. My body flew back and landed hard on the pavement.

"*What the fuck!*" I heard Drake through the ringing in my ears.

My face felt like it was on fire so I ran my hands up and down it feverishly. When I was sure I was good, I opened my eyes slowly. The debris from the explosion made the air thick. I pushed myself off the ground, staggering a little before gaining my balance. Deidra's car was still in flames as I approached it with a heavy heart.

"My sister!" Drake hollered.

TO BE CONTINUED...

Made in the USA
Columbia, SC
26 March 2021